행복

VEN. POMNYUN SUNIM

BECOMING HAPPIER

BECOMING HAPPIER
We Can Choose to Be Happy at Any Moment

First Edition	October 20, 2022
Second Edition	January 10, 2025

Published by	Jungto Publishing
	42 Hyoryeong-ro 51-gil, Seocho-gu, Seoul, Korea
	tel. +82-2-587-8991
	e-mail. jungtobook@gmail.com
Written by	Ven. Pomnyun Sunim
Translated by	Jungto International Translation Team
Design by	Design Studio Dongkyeong

ISBN: 979-11-87297-45-1 (03810)
Printed in the Republic of Korea.

US $27 ₩20,000

VEN. POMNYUN SUNIM

Becoming Happier

We Can Choose to Be Happy at Any Moment

JUNGTO

I am the one who creates my own happiness.
I am the one who creates my own unhappiness.
Nobody creates my happiness
or unhappiness except for me.

You Have
the Right to Be Happy
Regardless of Your Life Situation

In my Dharma talks, I often ask people: "Are you happy?" Few answer "yes." They suffer from personal worries, emotional wounds, relationship conflicts, frustration, and stress developed from the irrational society we live in or anxiety about the future.

All kinds of events happen in our lives, and things usually don't turn out the way we want them to. We want to be loved, but instead, we may end up getting hurt. The people we care about may even betray us. Nothing happens without a reason, but the reason is not the result of God's will or even a sin committed in a previous life. We simply don't know the reason why things turn out the way they do. But if we could identify where our suffering comes from, we could easily find a way to overcome it and free ourselves from suffering entirely.

A big part of our unhappiness comes from our inability to let go. Imagine, for example, that a stranger swears at us. This is much the same as someone handing us a bag of rotten trash. For some reason, we tend to hold onto the bag tightly, rummaging through its contents for the rest of our lives. We say to ourselves, "That person swore at me, slighted me, and harmed me."

When we cling to such negative feelings, we can never enter the path to happiness. If someone were to give us a bag of actual, physical trash, we would certainly refuse to take it. If we were to take it by mistake, we would most likely say, "Ugh, this is filth" and immediately throw it away. Unfortunately, with various types of insults or harm, we continue to hold those negative feelings deep in our hearts, which makes it difficult for us to be happy no matter how hard we try.

There are many obstacles to being happy, such as

unfulfilled desires, bad habits, living in an unfair society, or our own thoughts. If we suffer from negative thoughts, it would be best to change this habit of negative thinking. If we suffer from a relationship that has gone sour, we should examine the cause of the failure. If we believe that our social system is the problem, it would be best to start by trying to adapt to the current system. If we are certain that society is, in fact, the actual source of our problems, we should try to improve it. However, most of us just continue to complain without making any real effort to change our surroundings. As a result, the world doesn't change, and we continue to be miserable.

Anybody who is born into this world has a right to be happy. For more than thirty years, I have mainly focused on how individuals should cultivate positive attitudes through practice, as a way of affecting change for those who do not exercise this right to be happy and are mired in suffering. In this book, I will also talk about social change, another wheel on the cart of happiness. Ultimately, our happiness will be whole and complete only when our individual, internal mental attitudes – the seeds of happiness and fulfillment – and external social conditions – the field in which these seeds are sown – are cultivated together.

Achieving individual happiness and creating a decent and just society are not two separate, distinct things. An individual's lone effort doesn't make the world a better place; improved external conditions alone cannot make an individual happy. Happiness and unhappiness are the combined result of an individual's mental attitudes and the surrounding environment that individual inhabits. We need to reflect on ourselves before blaming others for our problems, and simultaneously take responsibility for improving the irrational parts of the present reality within which we find ourselves. In the end, it's all to our benefit. No matter how ardently and sincerely we may try to lead a good life, each of us is bound to suffer when things go wrong in the world around us. Complacent thoughts like "As long as it's not me being harmed, it's all right" or "That couldn't possibly happen to me" will not protect us.

To enter the path to complete happiness, we must become the masters of our own lives and become aware that we are responsible for our own happiness. Each of us is an insignificant entity, a speck of dust floating in space, but when we become the masters of our own lives, we can change ourselves and our world.

When we aspire to make the world a better place for all rather than trying to lead a good life only for our own benefit, we will simultaneously become happy within ourselves and helpful to the larger world. Happiness will be a reality rather than a dream. Being helpful to the world results in our own personal happiness. My hope is that this book will be a guide to happiness for those of you who are tired of living, who have been hurt by relationships, or who suffer needlessly in this seemingly irrational world.

Oct., 2022.
Ven. Pomnyun Sunim

Contents

Part 03 /

How to Live with People Who
Have Different Opinions from Yours

Part 04 /

Do Not Build Your Happiness
on Other People's Misfortune

Part 05 /

Practice Being Happier Today
Than Yesterday

PART 01

WHY DOESN'T LIFE TURN OUT THE WAY WE WANT IT TO?

Several people waiting for the bus at the station will each have different thoughts going through their heads. One may be feeling hurried and anxious. They may be thinking, "Why isn't the bus here already?" Another may be blaming someone else for their own hurried, anxious state of mind. Their thought might be, "I would have caught the last bus if I hadn't been cornered and nagged while I was trying to get ready this morning." A third person may be consumed by a completely different worry, thinking, "Since the bus is taking so long to come, it's bound to be extremely crowded."

In contrast to people whose mental habit is to dwell upon such negative thoughts, there are also those who maintain a positive attitude. They will likely wait patiently. They may be thinking to themselves, "It's not like the bus will arrive any sooner if I fret and worry about it." When the bus finally arrives, but is uncomfortably crowded, they may think, "Thank goodness I was able to get on the bus even if I can't sit down."

Most of our lives consist of a continuous stream of such moments. Sadly, we waste much of our precious time feeling anxious and fretful in the moment and experiencing regrets later.

When we encounter difficulties, we fail to live in the present because we wish for things to get better in the future. Even when everything is going fine, we become anxious that something bad may happen to disrupt our peace. Thus, we fail to enjoy even a moment of true happiness as time races past us.

Choice and
Self-Contradiction

Over the course of our lives, we make the choices that we think are best at the time based on the information we have. Looking back, however, we often realize that the choices we considered to be good at the time did not lead to the best outcomes. You may get married to be happy, but your marriage could end up making you unhappy. You might have a child, expecting that this will lead to fulfillment, but your child may very well make you feel so miserable that you envy people who never had any children in the first place. You start a business to make money, but you end up in debt.

We often feel regret and misery because things don't turn

out the way we intended. Then, we are left to wonder if we are truly the masters of our own lives or have been swept up by the currents in the world. Are we actually living as masters of our own lives?

Once there was a man who hoped to attain enlightenment, so he left his home, his assets, his position, and his loved ones in order to become a monk. After years of practice at a temple, he came to believe that it would be impossible to attain enlightenment if he continued to live in a community of monks. He felt he didn't have enough time to practice because he had to do chores, cook meals, and perform the various tasks that were part of communal living. He thought to himself that it would be better to go alone, deep into the mountains, where he could practice becoming enlightened uninterrupted, to his heart's content.

He traveled deep into the mountains, to a spot about ten kilometers from the nearest village, where he built a thatched cottage to shelter him from the elements. He walked down to the village to get food. The man found that he had to do even more labor now than he'd had to do at the monastery. The cottage needed frequent repairs, and almost every day, he had to make the ten-kilometer trek to the village to get food. Furthermore, walking such long distances required him to make straw shoes more often than before. He found that he had no time at all to practice.

To make matters worse, he soon became sick. He went to a doctor, who told him that his illness was caused by malnutrition. So, to regain his strength, he would need to drink a glass of milk every day. But walking down to the village every day to get his glass of milk was too time-consuming, so he bought a pair of goats.

Owning the goats spared him the trouble of making a daily trip to the village, but it led to even more chores. He had to tie the goats to posts to prevent them from wandering off. He had to cut enough grass to feed them. The acquisition of the goats allowed him to drink the milk he needed for his health, but tending to their needs left him with even less time to practice. In order to solve this new problem, he hired a goatherd.

Now he needed to pay the one who tended his goats. Previously, during his alms round, he only had to obtain enough food to feed himself. But now he also had to get food and money for the goatherd, so his alms round took up much more time. He knew he couldn't go on this way.

He thought that perhaps it might be better for him to marry than to continue this way. So, he got married. He was so relieved that he didn't have to pay the goat keeper anymore or do any housework. He thought that he could finally concentrate on his practice. But alas, his new wife became pregnant.

So, the man who had left his home and family to become a monk and to attain enlightenment ended up getting married, having children, and scraping a living together the same as any other layperson.

Hearing this man's life story, you might think of him as very foolish. But most of us live our lives in the same way. We think that all the choices we make are good, but looking back we can see that, tempted by the prospect of a moment's comfort and ease, we forgot our initial goal and purpose. If a man gets married, he should live accordingly. If a man leaves home to become a monk, he should also live accordingly. If we were to keep such a clear perspective on life, we would suffer less, but we are so easily swayed when things get tough. Suffering from daily life, we might say, "Maybe I should become a monk." Then, after becoming a monk, we might envy a layman's life and find ourselves thinking, "This practice is too hard."

We may also do foolish things, like the Buddhist monk in the story who lost track of his initial goal. Faced with this reality, we have two options. One is to forget about our initial goals and live according to the situation in which we find ourselves. There is really nothing wrong with that. The other option is to return to our initial goal the moment we realize that we have deviated from it.

Out of habit, people say things like, "I will be happy when I have enough money," or "I'll be happy when I find a life partner." But then, they make money or get married, and they still aren't happy. When they don't have children, they think they'll be happier when they have a child. But then, once they have a child, they become convinced that they will be happy when their child goes to elementary school, and they'll have more free time. Next, they think they'll be happy when their child goes to middle school, and then they believe that happiness will arrive when their child finally moves out of the house and goes to college. When the child does go to college, they still continue to postpone their happiness, believing that they will be happy when their child gets a good job, then when their child gets married, then when they have a grandchild, or when their grandchild grows up and becomes independent. Throughout their lives, people keep changing the conditions they think they need to be happy. As a result, they may die without ever having tasted happiness.

Wealth, fame, family, friends, and the like are not the cause of suffering, nor are they the ingredients for happiness. Sometimes, we think these things make us happy; at other times, we think they make us suffer. If we go back and forth between these two extremes, we will never be free from suffering.

If you're married, instead of being dissatisfied and worrying, it would be better to think, "I have a spouse, a house, and a job. I have nothing in the world to envy. My life is the best."

If we accept our life as it's, we will become free and happy. If we have a goal that we want to achieve, we have to stop the habit of running forward blindly toward that goal. Also, rather than resolving to change our behavior starting tomorrow, or perhaps the day after tomorrow, we have to learn to be happy here and now.

In life, there is no single answer that will always be the right choice. We live as we choose to. But we hesitate when making choices because we don't want to be responsible for unwanted consequences.

We can't say for certain that life is good or bad. There are only choices and the responsibilities that come with the choices we make. Taking responsibility for the choices we make involves the ability to willingly accept the consequences of those choices. If we truly accept the consequences of our actions, we won't be miserable or resentful, no matter what the outcome.

Between the Ideal
and the Real

Sometimes, we feel that we are lagging behind, left out, while others pursue their dreams and live their lives to the fullest. Our inner conflict is amplified when we have dreams we want to fulfill and things we want to do but are forced to give them up because of various life circumstances.

A person in their thirties might complain that they had to give up their dreams in order to make a living, and they may feel very unhappy because of this reality. "If I had the means," they might complain, "I would resume my studies in design, but I'm married and have a child, so it's too hard to quit my job and pursue that dream." They would likely end up wondering if it's right to abandon their dream and just live like they do.

Many of us believe that we'd be happy if we had the job for which we have the greatest aptitude. Aptitude matters for some jobs, but it doesn't for others. It was my own dream to become a scientist, and I thought that I had an aptitude for it. I never even imagined becoming a monk. You can imagine how much torment and inner conflict I have experienced over the years, living as a Buddhist monk rather than as a scientist.

Since leaving home at 16 to live as a monk, I've tried to apply scientific thinking to my life in a new way. I didn't believe in the baseless precepts of religion, so I distanced myself from them. I thought hard about the question, "What can I do to help people understand the Buddha's teaching more easily?" This is why, in my Dharma talks, I try to deliver the Buddha's teaching coherently and logically. No matter what kind of work you do, it will always be affected by your personal inclination.

Believing you have an aptitude for science, you may come to believe that you need to have a job related to science in order to be fulfilled in your work. This is a fixed notion. You can't be sure that your aptitude will only fit the specific jobs you have in mind. So, when you do your best, you can use your talents and abilities in any job you perform.

I often tell young people who are looking for a job to do what they really want to do. I tell them to do what makes their heart beat faster. Young job seekers should think carefully about the true meaning of these words. They should search for jobs that suit them personally rather than pursuing professions that promise money, social status, power, or security. If someone discovers a job that they really find appealing and believe they would be good at, they should pursue it even if it doesn't initially make them a lot of money rather than wasting time worrying about whether or not it's a "good" job. The occupations that we label as "good" are not necessarily good for everyone. One should not blindly follow a career path just because a majority of people recommend it as "good."

That said, you likewise don't need to torment yourself with questions like, "Why don't I have a passion for anything?" or "Why don't I have something that I would like to devote my life to?" In the world, there are those who have a passion for one particular thing, and there are those who don't. It

BECOMING HAPPIER

may even be better not to have a passion for one particular thing because then you can be content with whatever work is given to you. This would have the effect of making you more free. Those on the highest level of enlightenment live this way – cooking when cooking needs to be done, doing laundry when laundry needs washing, giving a lecture when a lecture needs to be given, and doing farm work when farm work needs doing.

One can actually become free by not insisting on the one and only way that they feel is right. Most people cannot attain such freedom, so they try to focus on at least one thing and try to do it well. Thus, right now, you don't really have to worry about not wanting to do anything with passion or liking anything in particular.

Moreover, you shouldn't despair about not being able to do the one thing that you want to do. You may want to study design, but your current situation might not allow it. In that case, you can try to incorporate the ideas and principles of design into your current work, instead of agonizing over not being able to pursue design as an independent career any further.

Let's say you become a monk. Wouldn't you still have the

opportunity to practice design? You could become interested in the design of monks' robes, the layout of the monastery garden, or study the modernization of temple designs that preserve the structures' traditional beauty. It's not really important what kind of work you do. If you work on what happens to come your way, you will be able to find your aptitude and employ your talent.

Ignoring your present reality while searching for your dream, and pursuing future happiness, is like building a castle in the air. But focusing only on making a living in the present will leave you without hope for the future. People agonize over whether to pursue their ideals or focus on their present circumstances. However, the relationship between future ideals and present reality does not need to be in perpetual conflict. Plant your feet firmly in reality, while your eyes look toward your ideals.

Thirty years ago, I opened a Dharma center. My aspiration was to break away from the common practice of seeking good fortune, and instead focus on studying the Buddha's original teachings and attaining enlightenment. Prior to opening the center, I tried to adapt this aspiration to a Korean Buddhist temple, which led to a lot of conflicts. At that temple, it was customary to pray for blessings and perform ancestral rites in order to receive good fortune, but I refused to participate. People complained about me to the abbot. They said, "If this monk continues to do that, we will lose all our lay Buddhists."

I had no choice but to leave the temple and open a small Dharma center where I started to spread the Buddha's teaching. Did many people recognize my good intentions and come to the center? No, they didn't.

At first, I handed out leaflets that read, "I have opened a Dharma center. Please, come to study the Buddha's teachings." About ten people came to the center, but after a disappointed look around the tiny center, they left and never came back. Still, I didn't give up and kept handing out leaflets.

I prepared a three-month Buddhist lecture program and invited a famous monk to the opening ceremony. Five people came that day, but after the first lecture, only one remained. After planning a three-month course of study and seeing such poor attendance, I'm sure most people would have canceled the program. I delivered the lecture series to the one remaining student for the entire three months.

After the program ended, the one person who had attended brought several acquaintances to the Dharma center. After handing out more leaflets, ten more people came and five stayed. I gave the three-month lecture to these new students. That is how the Dharma center slowly grew, to become the Jungto Society of today.

I was penniless at the time, so how was I able to keep the Dharma center open? On the days I didn't give lectures, I worked part-time at a local academy as a math instructor, and I used the money I earned there to cover the expenses of running the center. I continued doing this for the next four years and only stopped once the Dharma center finally became financially independent.

If I had compromised because of the difficult situation, I wouldn't have been able to take the path I wanted to follow. Even when we are sure of our dream for the future, we sometimes feel doubtful and ask ourselves if we are on the right path. At times like these, we need to work hard in the present, while simultaneously thinking about how things could be in ten years' time. We should study ways to face each day's challenges.

Simply waiting will not bring about a positive future.

We make our dreams for the future into a present reality by investigating ways to realize them and overcoming challenges.

Walk Out of the Prison
of the False Sense of Self

People complain about the world not going their way. Are they satisfied with themselves? No. It seems that most people, while not happy with the way the world is going, are not satisfied with themselves either. Even those who appear to be free of problems, and seem to live in enviable circumstances, often feel this ongoing sense of dissatisfaction. Why is that?

When we are not satisfied with ourselves, the reason isn't that we're not good enough but because we have such high expectations for ourselves. The dissatisfaction we experience is the result of our not meeting these high expectations.

We feel that we're not good enough. We think we are,

or should be, exceptional people. Fixated on this image of ourselves, we consider ourselves superior to others, but when we fail to meet this unrealistic self-image, we feel frustrated. Thus, we oscillate between blaming others for our frustration and blaming ourselves for our own incompetence.

A man once asked me for advice: He felt resentful for having been born into a poor family but also felt guilty for having such thoughts. "All my life," he said, "I've blamed my family's poverty on parental incompetence. After I started to practice, I stopped blaming my parents. I felt apologetic toward them for my resentment, and I have repented a great deal. Now I feel unhappy about myself and feel depressed and guilty. I've begun to blame myself. How can I accept myself as I am?"

If you have repented about previously resenting your parents, tell yourself that your parents have given you so much and that it was foolish to resent them, but you should stop right there. If you blame yourself for having resented your parents, you're just changing the target of your resentment from your parents to yourself. That is not the solution.

Just as blaming your parents is not the attitude of a practitioner, neither is clinging to your past foolishness and continuously berating yourself for your actions. If you continue to blame yourself, you will feel despondent. If these feelings worsen, you will fall into a depression.

Depression is like a deep swamp. Once you are seized by a certain thought, it will engulf you quickly, and it will feel utterly real. At such times, shake your head and work to escape from the quagmire of such ideas. If you feel depressed while sitting, stand up and move around to change your mood. Take a bath, take a walk, do stretches, or do manual work. Get yourself out of that quagmire, so you do not revert back to harboring depressing thoughts.

We think we have made progress only when we reach the standards set by our egos. But this expectation is not to your benefit. If you think that way, it will be too hard for you to feel satisfied with yourself. Happiness starts with accepting yourself as you are. You need to acknowledge your current state and find a way to be positive about it.

If you fall down, you are the one falling. If you get angry, you are the one getting angry. We think of ourselves as the kind of people who don't stumble or lose our temper, so it's painful to watch ourselves when we do. Since we cling to the self-image that we have formed, we become displeased. We are so full of our false sense of self that we feel ashamed of our real selves.

Your real self is neither good nor bad, but if your self-image seems better to you than your real self, then you'll feel you are not good enough. If your self-image is worse than your real self, you'll feel that you are someone special.

When your self-image is too high, you can't tolerate your real self. As a result, you may blame yourself for failing to live up to the image. You can be mentally healthy only when your self-image isn't too different from your real self. This is why mentally healthy people do not despair, even in the face of difficulties.

When we think, "I don't seem to know much about this problem. I'll study it and overcome it," we can accept and think positively about ourselves and make a little more effort to change. But if you have a self-image that is much better than your real self, you can't satisfy yourself no matter how hard you try. In the end, you will despair and think, "I am useless."

In short, the level of your happiness varies greatly depending on how you see yourself. What happens if you think that you can run 100 meters in 13 seconds, when in reality, it actually takes you 20 seconds? Running the 100 meters in 20 seconds might not be a problem, but if you can't make it in 13 seconds no matter how hard you try, you will blame yourself and think only about how useless you are.

Feeling insecure or inferior comes from delusions of grandeur. Your conceit and false perceptions about your life as overly significant makes you miserable. There is no special meaning to existence. As they learn this, some people ask me if there is any reason to live, or they say, "Isn't it sad to live in this world if existence has no meaning?"

All beings, including human beings, have no special meaning. Meaning is created by human consciousness. Concepts such as valuable and worthless, virtuous and evil, good and bad, heaven and hell, the Buddha and God, are all created by human consciousness.

Just as the caterpillar locks itself in the cocoon it has spun, humans imprison themselves in the concepts they have created. Charcoal and diamonds, both made of carbon, have no intrinsic value; people have arbitrarily assigned value to them. When the weather is so cold that you could freeze to death, charcoal is more valuable than diamonds. People are miserable when they try to shine like diamonds, but if they change their views and aspire to be useful like charcoal, they can lead worthwhile lives.

The same is true when people evaluate others. If someone who doesn't know anything about me comes to my Dharma talk without any expectations, they might walk away thinking, "Wow, he's great." Perhaps they thought my ability was about 50, but after listening to my Dharma talk, they decided that my ability is closer to 100, so their evaluation is very positive.

Someone else might attend my Dharma talk after having heard that I am a renowned monk and come expecting my ability to be 150. After listening to my talk and deciding I don't meet these high expectations, they will probably say something like, "There was nothing special in his talk. What's all the fuss about?" My ability is still 100, but the listener with low expectations will be more satisfied, whereas the one with high expectations will be less satisfied.

Sometimes, we look at someone else's behavior and think to ourselves, "Why on earth would they do that?" We feel frustrated about this other person because their actions do not fit the specific image we have created for them. Based on our own standards, their behavior might seem unsatisfactory or wrong. But the truth is that the standard against which we are measuring them is an illusion.

You might think that your spouse should be a certain type of person or that your child should act a certain way. Your family disappoints you because you measure them against the images you have created for them. Just as we should not expect too much of ourselves, in order to be happy, we should not expect too much of others and should accept them as they are.

The fact is that you are not all that special, and neither are others. If you feel dissatisfied with others because they don't meet your standards, the problem is not theirs but yours. Your level of expectation is the problem.

You need to walk out of the prison formed by your false sense of self. Instead of making a resolution to be a certain way, become aware that regrets and self-blaming come from an illusory sense of self. This awareness is the first step to freeing yourself.

Just become aware of yourself, that's all. Don't hate yourself. If you hate yourself for making mistakes, you have foolishly defined yourself as someone who must not ever make any mistakes. Forgive yourself for making mistakes, just as you should forgive others for making mistakes.

When you fall, get right back up and continue on your way. Rather than blaming yourself for falling, try your best not to fall again. Starting today, you can practice acknowledging and accepting yourself as you are. Be generous to yourself. Then, you will gradually and naturally become kinder to others.

All beings in the world are neither perfect nor imperfect. Because we like to think we're special, we paradoxically feel worthless and small. Human beings, animals, grass, and stones are all just beings. Humans are animals, not all that different from squirrels and rabbits. Human consciousness is just a little more developed than that of other animals.

Squirrels and rabbits don't suffer due to thoughts, so it seems wrong for humans to suffer with the thought that life is hard. Imagine how shackled humans must feel if they envy a bird's ability to fly.

We are just like the grass and the ants. We are insignificant, but, in reality, we are also precious. When we realize this, we can live peacefully without caring about what others think of us, and without interfering in other people's lives.

The Secret to
Happiness

One day, a lay Buddhist said to me, "I have made donations to temples countless times, but it has not brought me any blessings. If it was guaranteed that donating $1 would return $100 in value to me, I would donate so much more."

Wanting to get $100 in return for donating $1 at a temple is no different from gambling in a casino. Even without praying for material rewards, the things that people ask for in prayers offered to the Buddha at a big temple are sometimes just as absurd. People wish to gain a great deal with minimal effort. For instance, they pray for their child, who has poor grades and does not work hard in school, to be admitted to a good college.

If you pray this way, you are bound to invite misfortune. The desire to work a little and receive a lot is the mindset of a thief. This outcome requires that someone else has to sacrifice in your stead. For example, should your child who has poor grades and does not work hard be admitted to a good college, someone else's child who has better grades may be denied admittance to that college.

It makes perfect sense that such prayers should go unanswered, but people don't think that what they're asking for is unreasonable. Instead, they end up blaming the Buddha or God.

People usually pray for the things they think are hard to achieve on their own, which makes it very unlikely that their prayers will be answered. As a result, their lives are filled with more pain than joy.

It would be nice if everything went our way, but in reality, it doesn't. The belief that if we want something badly enough it will come true is delusional and greedy. When something we want doesn't come true, it's our choice whether to be unhappy, crying, and clinging to what we want, or to live happily despite the reality.

Must our lives be miserable if what we want doesn't come true? No. We suffer because we believe that what we wish for should come true. If we stop thinking this way, everything will be just fine, whether our wishes are fulfilled or not.

Even when we work hard to achieve what we want, things don't always turn out the way we had hoped or expected. The result of our work is influenced by our own efforts, as well as the circumstances around us. When we understand this, we can avoid the feeling of being greatly disappointed when we don't achieve what we want.

Mistakes and even despair can actually make us stronger. When plants keep growing upward without being pruned or trimmed, they grow leggy, fail to bear fruit, and are easily broken.

Whether what we want comes true or not, we can experience happiness in the process of working toward it. Most of us think that we can be happy and free only when everything turns out the way we want it to, but this is virtually impossible. Sometimes, external circumstances make it possible for things to go our way, and other times, they make it unlikely. If our own happiness is dependent on external conditions or circumstances, we can never be completely happy. Still, we cling to the desire that things should turn out the way we want, so naturally, we are sometimes unhappy.

Consider a farmer who spends an entire evening preparing to spray pesticide on his fields early the next morning. Since pesticides can't be sprayed on rainy days, he prays to the Buddha before he goes to sleep: "Dear Lord Buddha, I'm going to spray pesticide tomorrow, so please don't let it rain."

Waking up to rain, he complains to himself, "Well, I was going to spray pesticide today. The weather has been fine all week, and of all days, it rains today! It's no use praying to the Buddha."

Annoyed, he starts drinking. After a while, he begins to feel better and decides that since there isn't anything he can do about the falling rain, he will spend the following day planting pepper seedlings. Before going to sleep, he prays to the Buddha again: "Dear Lord Buddha, now that it's raining, let it continue to rain tomorrow."

He wakes up to find that the weather has cleared and again becomes angry. "What the hell is wrong with the weather? It's sunny when I want it to rain, and it rains when I want it to be sunny. How can I work if the weather is going to be so fickle? This is impossible." Once again, he starts drinking.

If the farmer acts this way, blaming the weather, he will inevitably ruin his crops. Likewise, blaming other people and circumstances, "I can't be happy because of my child," or "I can't be happy because of my husband," or "I can't be happy because of my boss," will ruin your life.

What kind of attitude would benefit the farmer the most? At night, he should go to sleep peacefully. If the weather is favorable when he wakes up after a good night's sleep, he can prepare to spray pesticide. If it drizzled instead, he could plant the pepper seedlings. If the rain is torrential, he should take a break, reminding himself that he'd been working very hard lately and should have a drink and spend the day resting.

It's difficult for a farmer to do his job if he can't let go of his fixed expectations and wants. it's just so with our lives. Our environment changes constantly. If we can't let go of expectations and desires about how things should be, we will be in a constant state of suffering. We'll be controlled by the unpredictable changes in our environment.

If we set the conditions for our happiness in advance, and then insist on them, our prospects for happiness will drift away. If we let go of our insistence on everything going our way, and deal wisely with the circumstances as they are, happiness will naturally follow.

Despite this obvious truth, people demand to know the special secret to obtaining happiness without letting go of their insistence on obtaining it. Why? Because rather than letting go of high expectations, they crave more. They want so many things, and unfortunately, they often believe they will get what they want more quickly if they do things a certain way, according to one specific plan that they have in mind.

Imagine a person is holding a firebrand, a burning piece of wood which represents their expectations and desires, in their left hand. They scream that it's hot. I would tell that person something like, "If it's hot, let go of it."

This person might ask me, "How can I let go of it? Tell me how."

Is this person asking because they really don't know how to physically let go of the firebrand? Not really. They say that they want to let it drop, but actually, they don't want to let go, and so they continue to ask me how it's possible to drop it. There is only one answer I can give: "Just let go." They ask again: "How can I just let go?"

This person will say that Buddhism is very difficult and unrealistic, and they may complain that instead of teaching them how to let go of the fireball, I just keep telling them to let it go. This problem can't be solved because they want someone else to fix the problem while avoiding acknowledging that they are the one holding onto it. So, I'm forced to tell them to move the firebrand to their right hand instead. Their expression brightens, and they say, "You should have told me about this terrific solution earlier!"

But will they be able to hold it in their right hand? No, not for long. Soon, they'll cry out that their right hand is now burning. They're holding onto it, not because they don't know how to let it go, but because they don't really want to. Unable to let go of attachment to the firebrand, this person continues to hold it while screaming in pain.

Moving the firebrand from the left hand to the right and back again satisfies two purposes: It momentarily relieves the burning sensation and allows the person to continue to hold onto the firebrand. This may seem like a good solution, but it's not the fundamental way to be free from suffering.

Most people just try to avoid the immediate burning

sensation because they don't want to let go of what is burning them. When I tell them, "Just drop it," they tell me that this is not very realistic. When I tell them, "Move it to your left hand," they say, "What a good idea," but in the end, they'll feel the same burning sensation all over again.

Moving the firebrand from the right hand to the left is only a temporary solution. To be happy, you have to let go of it as soon as you feel the heat. Even knowing this, you may still occasionally suffer because you've developed the habit of holding on to it. Those who understand that they just need to let go do not suffer for very long. They only suffer momentarily when they become attached to something, but since they know they just have to let go, the suffering is short-lived. These are wise people who have changed from their former selves.

Setting an Aspiration
After Letting Go of Greed

A doctor once asked me for advice. He wanted to give up his difficult and exhausting job in medicine and relocate to somewhere far away. "When I first began working as a doctor," he said, "I thought it was my vocation because it was rewarding to treat sick people. Many people think highly of doctors, and it pays well. However, I'm barely able to put up with the work each day. I'm afraid of medical accidents, and working is no longer fun for me, so I want to give up my practice and move abroad. But it's difficult to decide what to do because my daughter is only four years old."

Buddhism tells people to let go of greed, but people

mistakenly think that letting go means avoiding all of the suffering in their lives.

So, what is the difference between letting go and evading reality? The biggest difference lies in the resulting consequences. When we let go, the same problem doesn't occur again, but when we evade reality, it does. If a man drinks every night to forget the pain of a breakup, he may momentarily escape from his pain, but when he sobers up, he'll feel it again. If, however, he lets go of his attachment to his former partner and instead thinks, "Thank you for the time you spent with me. Goodbye," he will no longer suffer. Letting go solves a problem; evading reality does not.

If a person doesn't have a good relationship with their parents and keeps avoiding their calls, the conflict they have with them, and the suffering that comes with it, will continue. By letting go of resistance to answering the parents' calls, the suffering will disappear. Willingly answering the calls from the parents makes the calls no longer feel like a burden.

Even when it seems that a problem has been solved by letting go of our attachment, the problem may occasionally reoccur. This happens when our mind once again dwells on the problem. However, since we have already let go of the attachment, we can overcome the problem more easily.

When instead we evade a problem by suppressing our feelings, it will grow worse over time. We may repress our feelings once, twice, three times, but eventually, we will explode with anger. When a problem occurs, it's better to face it head-on and solve it rather than to evade it.

If the doctor who asked me for advice leaves his job and moves to another country, he may feel lighthearted and peaceful at first. But the unresolved problem is likely to reoccur anytime, anywhere, and in any form.

In life, we find ourselves involved in four types of situations. The first is when we want to do something, and we can do it. The second is when we want to do something, but we can't do it. The third is when we don't want to do something, and we don't have to do it. The fourth is when we don't want to do something, but we have to do it.

In the first situation, it's easy to just go ahead and do it. In the third situation, we can simply avoid what we don't want to do. Thus, we can live approximately half our lives in exactly the way we want to. The problem is that we also find ourselves in the second and fourth situations, where we can't do what we want to, or we have to do what we don't want to do. If we follow our desires in either of these two situations, we are likely to bring misfortune upon ourselves. To avoid this outcome, we have to let go of our desire to do something if we know that it's something we shouldn't do. Likewise, if it's something we have to get done, we must let go of our aversion and take care of it. Letting go of the desire to do something, which we experience as "craving," or not wanting to do something, which we experience as "aversion" is, in Buddhism, referred to as "letting go of greed" or "emptying the mind."

People ask, "How can I let go of greed in these fiercely competitive times?" They may likewise say, "I let go of my greed, so my mind is at ease. But now I'm concerned about feeling aimless and apathetic."

Eating food when you're hungry is not greed. Sleeping when you are tired is not greed. Wearing warm clothes and seeking a warm place when you are cold is not greed. Greed is continuing to eat even when you're full. Greed is not sharing food with others who are starving.

Wanting wealth or power is not, in itself, greed. Greed is not defined by the things you want, be they large or small. Greed is the desire for that which stands in contradiction.

Greed means not wanting to repay a debt after borrowing money or wanting to withdraw a large sum of money without saving. Greed is the desire to be admitted to a good college without studying. Greed is the futile desire to want things to go your way when it's not possible.

We suffer when the things we want don't come to fruition. The cause of this suffering is greed. That is why Buddhism teaches us to let go of greed and replace it with something else: aspiration.

What, then, is the difference between greed and aspiration? If you feel distressed when things don't go your way, you're being greedy. If you put in 30% of the necessary effort but want the results of a 100% effort, your desire will not be realized. When you're being greedy, wanting a great deal after only offering minimal effort, you will feel miserable. Greed, rather than motivating or helping you, will hinder you from achieving your goal.

Those who have aspirations, and make the necessary effort to achieve their goals, don't feel distressed or disappointed even if they fail. Instead, they look for other ways to achieve their goals.

When a child learns how to ride a bike, they never succeed

in riding it right away; they have to practice. If a child gets annoyed after falling once or twice, they may complain that there is something wrong with the bike or blame themselves for their clumsiness. This is greed based on the desire for an easy outcome with minimal effort. In order to learn how to ride a bike, they have to go through the process of falling over and over again.

If the child doesn't give up and continues to try despite falling down and scraping their knees, we can say that the child has an aspiration to ride a bike. Wanting to ride a bike and trying until one succeeds is not greed.

Whether your aspiration is great or small, if you try hard to achieve it, your ability will grow. Even if you fail, you'll develop the power and the capability to eventually succeed.

If you try harder to achieve your goal, despite the growing obstacles, you have an aspiration. You can continue to work toward your goal saying, "Since I have run into this obstacle, I'll try a new strategy to overcome it."

A person who has an aspiration researches, analyzes and tries again. If they finally realize that they can't achieve it after all, they will leave off trying without regret no matter how much effort they put in. They will not feel disappointed, regret the decision to try, or experience despair.

Ultimately, letting go of greed does not mean that you shouldn't strive to be successful. If there is something you really want, you should try your best to attain it. When you make the effort to achieve your aspiration, life will be more enjoyable, and you'll be more energized. Then, you will be more likely to achieve further success.

Time Lag Between the Cause
and the Effect

One day, one of the Buddha's disciples asked the Buddha, "Lord Buddha, the Brahmans say that even if a person has done bad deeds during their life, if a Brahman prays for them with an offering to the gods, that person will be forgiven and will be sent to Heaven. Is that true?"

The Buddha picked up a stone and threw it into a nearby pond. Then he asked the disciple, "If the Brahmans pray, 'Stone, float up to the surface,' would it float up to the surface?"

Upon hearing the Buddha's question, the disciple realized how foolish his question was. It's not only one of nature's principles but a case of simple logic that one who performs good deeds receives good consequences and one who commits evil deeds receives bad consequences, just like heavy stones sink in water and buoyant oil floats on its surface. In Buddhism, this is called the Law of Causality.

We sometimes wonder whether the Law of Causality really applies to our lives. It seems that although we have lived well enough, bad things still happen to us, while those who have done many bad things seem to lead happy lives. It seems quite untrue that doing good deeds will be rewarded, while doing harm will be punished.

The Buddha said, "No one can escape from the consequences of their deeds, whether they hides in the remote mountains or the deep sea." It doesn't seem to be true in daily life, but if we look very carefully, we learn that the Law of Causality does hold.

For example, parents may feel that raising a child is too difficult. They might even become irritated and angry with their child, not realizing the effect their actions have on the child's psyche. The consequences of their harmful actions don't manifest themselves immediately, so it's hard for them to see the principle of cause and effect. Even though the consequences may not appear right away, they certainly will eventually. The result of their actions may not appear in the child until ten years later. At that point, the parents may feel that the consequences came out of nowhere.

Some consequences appear immediately, some appear in ten days, and others appear in ten years. Some consequences appear in our own lifetime, and some appear in the lives of our descendants. There are times when we ourselves receive the consequences of our parents' or our ancestors' deeds.

There is a time lag between a cause and its effect. We see this in nature. The shortest day of the year, the winter solstice, is December 22nd. It seems logical that this should also be the coldest day of the year, but the coldest day of the year is actually sometime in late January or early February, about a month later. The longest day of the year is June 22nd, but the hottest days of the year are usually in late July and early August. The reason for this is that it takes some time for the earth to warm up or cool down.

In the same way, there is a time lag between a deed and its consequence. If we experience unwanted consequences even though we perform good deeds, the reason is that we're experiencing the effects of the bad deeds we have already done, whereas the consequences of our good deeds have yet to manifest themselves in our lives.

If we start practicing today, will everything suddenly start to go well immediately today? Most likely not. Things may even get worse. This is not because we started to practice, but because we've done bad deeds in the past, for which we are only now receiving the consequences.

People don't know this principle, so when bad things happen to them despite their daily practice, they give up and stop practicing. This is like despairing that spring will never come when the weather gets colder after the winter solstice because of an expectation that the weather would warm up right away.

It's greedy to expect things to get better immediately after we start to practice. If we continue to practice for a hundred days, without expecting anything, we will get to know a little about ourselves:

"I am a little stubborn!"

"I get irritated often!"

"I am impatient!"

"I nag a lot!"

"I have a strong sense of right and wrong."

When we get to know a little bit about ourselves through practice, we will continue to practice every day, even though no one tells us to do so. If we continue to practice for one thousand days, others may notice some changes in us and tell us that we've changed.

The day we set an aspiration to begin practice can be compared to the winter solstice. The day we get to know a little about our karma through practice is like the start of spring, which is about a hundred days after the winter solstice. After a thousand days of practice, people may begin to tell us that we've changed, a point which can be compared to the peak of spring, when flowers are blooming everywhere. Just as we don't feel it's springtime until we see the flowers begin to bloom, people will not recognize we have changed until we've practiced for at least three years, even though we ourselves feel that we have changed for the better long before that.

Obviously, if people received negative consequences immediately after doing something bad, nobody would do bad deeds. But the consequences don't usually appear right away, so people are tempted to do bad things. Likewise, because we don't see the benefits of good deeds right away, we're often not motivated to continue doing them. That's why it's easy to do bad things and difficult to do good things.

Over time, the consequences of bad deeds can't be avoided, and the rewards for good deeds are bound to appear. Although good consequences do result from good deeds, they don't appear in the form and at the time we want them to. They arrive on their own time.

Thus, you shouldn't get too happy about avoiding the bad consequences of your bad actions. They are debts; you'll receive the consequences, sooner or later.

Be aware that there is a time lag between your deeds and their consequences. So don't expect some kind of boon right after doing a good deed. When you experience difficulties, accept them all as the negative consequences of your previous misdeeds.

When you do something for others, it's better to think that you are repaying old debts rather than accumulating merit. When we face difficult situations, we can easily overcome them by thinking, "I have a lot of debts, so I'm paying them back."

We need to do a lot of good deeds without thinking about the results. Over time, we will see good results with just a little bit of effort. These results are not gifts from the universe. They are the consequences of the good deeds we have performed previously.

PART 02

FEELINGS ARE FORMED HABITS

When and how do sensations arise? They arise the instant when our sensory organs that mediate sight, hearing, smell, taste, touch, or thought, meet their respective objects, just like a spark is produced when steel strikes flint. There are three types of sensations that can arise: pleasant, unpleasant, and neutral. These sensations result in either craving or aversion.

Why, then, do different people respond differently to the same situation? The smell of bean paste stew makes some people drool in anticipation and others grimace with revulsion. Those who have attended church since they were young feel uneasy about entering a Dharma Hall, because their karma produces an unpleasant response to the new and unfamiliar surroundings.

Similarly, those who have attended Buddhist temples since they were young may view Christian communal prayers as strange. But neither the church nor the temple is the actual source of these feelings. Individual responses are different because each person's karma is different.

The empty winter field looks desolate after the harvest, but when spring arrives, and the weather gets warm, green shoots sprout again. The fact that green shoots sprout tells us that although it appeared as if there was nothing in the field, there were seeds in the soil.

Our minds are the same. Though not visible on the outside, everyone has their own individual karma, which responds to external stimuli. The karma ingrained in our body and mind creates sensations in response to external stimuli, such as color, smell, and sound.

Freedom from
Likes and Dislikes

When our six sense organs (the six roots in Buddhism: eyes, ears, nose, tongue, body, and mind) come into contact with external conditions, we experience all kinds of emotions: joy, sadness, fear, and loneliness, etc. We experience heaven when we like or love someone or something; we experience hell when we hate or resent someone or something. How do these emotions that make us feel happy or unhappy arise?

An emotion arises instantly, just like the spark generated by steel striking flint. If you were to see a person dying in the street, you would feel unsettled even though you didn't know that person. You would feel sad. If the death was caused by an injustice, you would feel angry.

Because our emotions arise instantly in response to external stimuli, we mistakenly believe that we are born with them, and therefore conclude that they can't be changed because they are an inherent part of us. We shouldn't fixate on this idea and consider our emotions absolute. There is no objective substance to our likes and dislikes.

We might feel happy when looking at a flower. When we look at a rose and find it beautiful, we immediately feel good. This kind of feeling doesn't have any negative effects because we don't expect the rose to like us in return. We feel that the flower is beautiful, and that's all there is to it.

On the other hand, your heart pounds when you gaze at someone with whom you are infatuated. But you're also likely wondering whether that person shares your feelings. You think to yourself, "Does she like me as much as I like her?" or "How can I make him like me back?"

Since you have these thoughts, and want the other person to like you, you feel confused, and your heart pounds. Your pounding heart may be a sign of fear that the person might not like you back.

No matter how strongly you want the other person to like

you, you cannot make them like you. It's an illusion to think that if you adore someone, the feeling will be reciprocated. It's one thing for you to like someone, but it's a totally separate, unrelated thing for that person to like you in return. So, when your heart pounds in the presence of someone you like, recognize that you are most likely thinking, "I want them to like me" rather than just "I like them."

A woman once asked me for advice, saying that there was someone at work whom she didn't like, but the problem was that her face showed it. "I tend to draw a clear line between what I like and what I don't like," she said, "and I consider it part of my personality. However, frankly expressing my feelings at work hasn't helped me. Should I change?"

Everybody has likes and dislikes. You don't have to hide these feelings to be a good person. There is nothing wrong with expressing your likes and dislikes. However, you should understand that if you are pushed around by your feelings, you will be imprisoned by them, and this is detrimental to you.

Our likes and dislikes come from our karma, that is, karmic consciousness. Consider the person who drools over the smell of bean paste stew but feels nauseous at the smell of curry. The latter response is a resistance to something not previously experienced and, thus, unfamiliar. A certain stimulus does not produce the same exact feelings in everyone, whether pleasant or unpleasant.

Feeling hungry when smelling bean paste stew or feeling disgust at the smell of curry are responses that arise from our karmic consciousness. We tend to think that the goodness or badness of something is inherent to the object itself, just like we believe that the odor of bean paste stew is delicious in itself, while that of curry itself is inherently disgusting.

The exact same color will look completely different, depending on the tint of the lenses you are wearing. You are, in this way, the one who determines your likes and dislikes. If you really know that feelings of attraction and aversion originate from within you, you will realize that arguing about likes and dislikes is pointless. Understanding this, you won't be carried away by the feelings that arise in you, even when you can't do anything to prevent them from happening.

If there is a person who thinks differently from you or who has a different point of view, there is no need for you to try to get to know them or to avoid them. But you shouldn't try to change them to suit you, either. You just need to accept them as they are.

Each of us lives according to our karma. Something that doesn't make any sense to you could make perfect sense to someone else. When dealing with the people in your life whom you can't avoid, accepting them as they are is the way to attain peace.

You'll be able to accept and understand others if you think to yourself, "How on earth could I change someone else's personality when I can't even change my own?" In this way, you will be able to live or work with people with whom you are not compatible.

Until now, you have suffered and complained because you thought that yours was the only right way. You probably thought that you had to live among those you love and had to part with those you hate. How free your life would be if you did not insist on your own likes and dislikes.

If you like kimchi and steamed rice, you can just eat them. Suppressing your desire to eat what you like is not practice. It's also fine for you to refrain from eating something you don't like. You might, however, have to live in a foreign country where you can't get kimchi or steamed rice. If you don't eat because there is nothing you like, your health will deteriorate. But if you eat too much of what you like, your stomach will expand, or you'll develop a stomach ache, which is also harmful. Therefore, there are times you have to eat something you don't like; there are also times you shouldn't eat something even though you like it.

If we like something, we believe that we must have it. And if we don't like something, we believe that we must get rid of it. We suffer because we find ourselves in situations where we can't get what we like or can't get rid of what we don't like. In these situations, it feels like we are in hell.

Therefore, if you're in a situation where you have to leave someone you like or must spend time with someone you don't like, don't let your likes and dislikes shackle you. Then, you will be freer in your life.

Anger, the Inner Fuse
That We Ourselves Ignite

Anger often leaves us feeling stressed and regretful. After expressing anger, we may feel ashamed about not having been able to control our emotions, or we may feel remorse over hurting someone. Why is it that we can't hold back our anger even though we know it will bring such undesirable results?

We get angry when we believe that we're right. We feel so right that others appear to be completely in the wrong. Such feelings lie deep in our subconscious. They don't surface easily, but they explode suddenly when we're with those who are closest to us, such as family members. After exploding in anger, we often say something like the following:

"I got angry without realizing it."

"I got angry out of habit."

"I got angry unconsciously."

These expressions signify that emotion is a habitual response from the subconsciousness.

But those who don't agree with this point of view might respond with something like "It was impossible not to get angry in that situation."

These seemingly objective standards are based on the value system or notions that were formed in the environment in which we grew up, and the experiences we have accumulated. The standards with which we judge whether a situation justifiably warrants our anger are completely subjective. We believe that our standards are objective, and thus fair, but they're actually the products of our own thoughts, preferences, and experiences.

When we get angry, it's not because of what someone else has said or done, but because we consider ourselves to be right and others to be wrong. Our habit of judging everything as right or wrong ignites the fuse inside us. Rather than the situation itself, what makes us angry is our thought that something did not meet standards that we consider to be "reasonable" or "objective." We judge people and situations according to our own standards. We get angry when they fail to meet them.

There is no absolute yardstick with which to judge something as right or wrong. Fundamentally, there is no right, and there is no wrong. Considering yourself as the standard causes others to be wrong. If you claim your standards are objective, you are proclaiming yourself to be absolutely right, and people will likely think of you as stubborn, self-righteous, or rigid.

Those who have a strong sense of right or wrong get angry easily. Those who are less rigid about what is right and what is wrong are less likely to get angry. When you let go of your subjective yardstick, there is no reason for you to insist that you are right or to criticize others. Then, you are not likely to get angry.

This doesn't imply that you should think that others are always right. It's not possible to say that your child who is addicted to video games or your husband who drinks constantly are right. You can, however, come to understand that the reason that your son and husband behave in this way is because of their own longtime habits. It's important to accept others as they are, before judging them based on your own thoughts and standards.

You might come home to find your child totally absorbed in playing computer games, not even acknowledging you as you walk in the door. You become very angry and shout. After acting out in anger, you are sorry and feel bad.

The next day, you come home from work to find your child playing computer games yet again. How will you react this time? Because you feel sorry about having shouted the day before, you try to suppress your anger and talk calmly. Your hesitation to yell or lecture isn't the result of thinking about what is best for your child. You hesitate because you're not sure which course of action is better for you – saying nothing and feeling frustrated or getting into an inevitable conflict when you do.

The child, however, is doing nothing more than playing computer games and having a good time. Because you view the child's actions based solely on your own thoughts and standards, you judge this behavior as a waste of time and get angry.

People generally think of suppressing anger as a good

thing, but venting anger and suppressing anger are more or less the same. In both cases, you're judging other people's actions based on your own standards. The only difference is whether or not you choose to express your emotion.

If you get angry because your child does not meet your standards, and scold them, you are just taking your anger out on the child. The child won't want to listen because they'll see this as nagging. You want to say something but decide to back off just this once.

Swallowing your anger is also not desirable because it will raise your stress level. Besides, suppressing your anger won't solve the problem. There is only so much you can put up with, so eventually, you will explode.

A man once asked me if getting angry at people who break social rules was justified. He told me, "I get angry at people who violate traffic signals when I'm driving. I want to chase the cars that cut in without signaling and get even. Those who do wrong should be punished in order for the world to function properly, shouldn't they?" Some people seem to think that getting angry about such behavior means they are somehow more justified than getting angry over personal matters.

There is something we need to consider first. Did the driver who cut in front of his car give him the anger that he experienced, or did the anger rise from inside the man himself? Let me give you a simpler example. If you feel sad looking at the moon rising over a hill, did the moon make you sad, or did looking at the moon make you sad? Some people feel joy when looking at the moon. Therefore, it's not the moon that makes people happy or sad. The emotion comes from within the minds of the people looking at the moon.

Let's apply this same principle to the man's road rage problem. If a car cuts him off when he is behind the wheel, did the anger arise from within the man himself, or did the driver in the other car make him angry? All we did was replace the moon with the other driver, yet people feel confused by this.

The confusion is resolved if we think about whether or not everyone in the same situation would get similarly angry. There are people who get angry when someone cuts them off while driving, and there are those who don't. Some drivers might just curse under their breath and keep driving, whereas others will express their anger by driving dangerously in retaliation or even go so far as resorting to violence.

In the end, we can see that there is no situation that always arouses anger in everyone. The cause of our anger lies within ourselves, so whether we get angry or not depends on how we respond to the situations we face.

In this world we all share, all kinds of things may happen, and all kinds of people exist. We can't meet or avoid all those whom we want to meet or avoid. To be free from suffering, we have to be constantly aware of how we discriminate between right or wrong, based on our karmic consciousness. We should practice letting go of our own standards, instead of imposing them on others. Then, no matter what situation we find ourselves in, or what kind of person we meet, we can prevent any unfortunate incidents caused by an inability to control our anger.

Neither Suppressing nor Venting Anger: A Third Path

When we get angry, we usually do one of two things: vent or repress it. We think of these as the only possible responses to anger, but there is a third way.

Recently, a woman asked me how to deal with her anger: "When I'm angry, I don't talk about it and tend to repress it. The cause of my anger seems too trivial to talk about, but it makes me angry not to say anything. Would it be better to just spit it out, or would I be better off to repress my anger, like I do now?"

If you vent your anger, the person you are angry with will probably also get angry, and the anger will expand. This makes venting the worst possible option. However, if you swallow your anger, the anger will not expand outward to others, but you are likely to get stressed and become ill, so this is also not a good choice. If you keep swallowing your anger, you might even suffer from symptoms such as a stiff neck, headache, and blurred vision.

Many women of our mothers' generation suffered from the symptoms of repressed anger. Sometimes a psychiatrist would incite the patient to vent their anger as an emergency treatment. By encouraging the patient to express their anger appropriately rather than continue holding it back, the symptoms would be somewhat alleviated.

However, this is just an emergency measure rather than a fundamental solution to the problem of anger. Like adding a bit of cold water to a boiling pot, it helps to momentarily suppress the energy, but the anger will inevitably boil over again.

Some believe that those who swallow their anger are better people because they don't express their negative emotions, but repressing anger does not make anyone happy. When you swallow your anger, you're more likely to experience stress and suffering, which is far from happiness, a state of being without suffering.

A Brahman once cursed the Buddha, accusing him of stealing one of his followers. When the Buddha didn't reply, the Brahman bragged that he had won an argument against the Buddha. Of this, the Buddha said, "Foolish people say they have won after cursing and slandering others. However, the real victory belongs to the one who knows the right way to respond. You should know that it's foolish to get angry at an angry person because that means you have been dragged into their emotions and lost to them. It also means that you could not control your own emotions, so you also lost to yourself, a double defeat."

The Buddha listened to the Brahman without saying a word, not because the Brahman was right, but because the Buddha understood that the Brahman's background and circumstances made it possible for him to say the things he said. The Buddha not only understood the Brahman's circumstances but also felt compassion toward him. Other people might wonder how the Buddha could endure such an insult, but the Buddha did not have to endure anything. He was able to stay calm because he fully understood and acknowledged the Brahman's situation.

When you reflect on the fundamental reason behind your anger, you are able to reach a state of being where anger doesn't arise. When you think "I am angry because of you," you need to think carefully about whether this is really true. Ask yourself the following:

"Why do I get angry when my child acts that way?"

"Why do I suffer when my spouse acts that way?"

"Why do I get stressed when my boss acts that way?"

You must be able to question the root of your own emotions. If you think critically before being swept away by these emotions, you may arrive at the conclusion that you have nothing to be angry about in the first place. You get angry, not because of your child, spouse, or boss, but because of yourself. You feel frustrated, miserable, or sad because you stubbornly insist on your own opinions, preferences, and thoughts.

However, after deeper introspection, you may discover that there is absolutely no reason or justification for your anger. As a result, you'll be able to reach a state where you don't get angry about anything.

We think of our emotions as real and inherent, but they are actually formed through our habits. When we are constantly being pushed around by our habits, they determine our fate. You get angry in the present because the seeds you have sown in the past have finally sprouted. If you continue to get angry, you will sow still more seeds that will bear negative fruit in the future.

Of course, it's not easy to see that there is never any reason to get angry no matter the situation, so we keep failing. But by continually trying to maintain awareness that anger arises from inside yourself rather than attempting to repress feelings of anger, you will find yourself getting angry less often.

If your habit is to get angry ten times a day, getting angry nine times a day is a success. If your habit has been to cling to your anger for more than an hour, you may find that your anger dissipates in under ten minutes once you acknowledge that you have become angry again.

It's easy to understand why we call an angry person "mad" when we look at their behavior. If someone were to threaten you with a knife, the most reasonable response would normally be to run away, but if you become very angry, you may lift up your shirt, thrust out your stomach, and shout something like "I dare you!" Obviously, at that point, you are not in your right state of mind.

Even though you may habitually get angry, if you remain aware of yourself and acknowledge that you are once again getting mad or throwing a fit all because you think you're right, you won't be carried away by your emotions. Just as the spark generated by a flint dies out in the absence of tinder, your anger will dissipate.

If you continue to do this, eventually you will become angry less often. Even if you fail to notice that you are getting angry at the exact moment the emotion arises, you can subsequently recognize that you failed to catch yourself. Instead of blaming some other person for your emotional state, you will find yourself gradually changing. You may get angry less frequently, and when you do become angry, the duration of your anger will become progressively shorter.

When someone gets angry at you, one way to avoid getting angry yourself is by responding with silence rather than immediately displaying your emotions. Once you've had a chance to calm down, try taking this a step further and smile when your husband, wife, child, parent, friend, or coworker rants at you.

At first, you'll fail 90% of the time. You may manage

to smile with your lips, but you won't be able to smile in your heart. Even so, force yourself to smile and try it again tomorrow, and the day after tomorrow. If you practice not being swept away by other people's emotions, you may eventually find yourself free from other people's actions.

When Feeling Indignant About Not Having Retorted to What Someone Said

If someone criticizes you unfairly or wrongly accuses you, but you are not able to say anything at the time, you may think to yourself later, "I should have said something."

At the moment, you couldn't think of anything to say. But later, things that you feel you should have said come to mind. A woman asked me for advice, saying that she felt resentful and furious about not having made a retort to someone: "Some time ago, I quarreled with a coworker, who lashed out at me in anger. But I couldn't think of anything to say because my mind went blank. Since then, I've felt increasingly regretful as I keep thinking of the things I should have said. How can I respond appropriately in those situations instead of behaving like a fool?"

If you want to think of something appropriate to say when you face a situation, you need to remain emotionally detached from the situation. You can't say something appropriate when you're embroiled in confrontation because you are too angry, resentful, distressed, or anxious to see things clearly. After you have calmed down, you may be able to think of all the things you should have said.

When someone swears at you, you are likely to get angry and swear back. Standing your ground may make you feel good in the moment, but you're likely to regret it later. If, on the other hand, you just repress your anger, you will feel like a fool.

If you are not seized by anger, you won't get entangled in another person's emotions. If you can gain enough understanding of the angry person and consider how awful they must be feeling to say such things, you might not become angry in return. You may even be able to say something comforting. Detach yourself from the situation. Getting angry in response to another person's anger means that you are being dragged down by their negative emotions.

Another method is to let go of your desire to "get even." You search for things to say because you want to defeat someone whom you see as an opponent. Later you feel resentful and angry because you couldn't think of anything to say that would win the verbal battle. I think what this particular questioner really wanted to ask me was something more like, "How can I defeat the other person verbally?"

In such a situation, the best way to become free is to rid yourself of the desire to defeat the person with whom you find yourself in contention. If you do find a way to win the verbal battle, you are likely to have accomplished this by hurting your "opponent's" feelings. If you hurt your own feelings, you can always repent when you realize that you've managed to hurt yourself. When you hurt someone else, there is no way to take back the injury, even if you repent your actions later on.

As an example, if your partner breaks up with you, you are likely to get angry. You may even feel that you should have dumped them first. If you do break up with someone, and later realize that you did something wrong, it would be difficult to rectify the situation. But if they break up with you, you may feel momentarily distressed, and your pride might be hurt. In this case, however, you just need to heal your own hurt feelings rather than also dealing with the guilt of having hurt someone else.

Wise people know it's better to get hurt themselves rather than to hurt someone else because ultimately the former entails less suffering than the latter.

Hating someone will not only distress you but will also rob you of the freedom to see that person because you will most likely try to avoid them. Hate acts like a mental restraining order. If we don't hate anyone, we can go anywhere freely and see anybody with ease.

Yet we keep imprisoning ourselves. To live freely, you must let go of your desire to defeat or get even with others, even if you believe that letting go of this desire will make you feel like a fool. It's better to look like a fool, than to keep going with your hate. The truly foolish are those people who act smart when they're not. Acting smart is a continual effort. Putting an end to a potentially confrontational situation by simply saying that you were wrong is much easier, since you don't have to rack your brain for just the right words to defeat the other person.

You never need to think of losing an argument as a defeat.

After all, you can only be defeated when you have a desire to win. If you have no desire to win, you will never be defeated.

Turning Old Wounds
into Life Assets

Surprisingly, we often get hurt by a family member or someone close to us. In most cases, however, we suffer because we remember something as having been hurtful, when it actually wasn't. Even hurtful things that happened a long time ago will continue to cause us to suffer because we can't let them go.

For instance, most people who say that their parents hurt them forget the many beneficial things that their parents did for them. They resent their parents in the present based only on their memories. They may say, "My parents sent my brother to college but not me," or, "Whenever my siblings and I would get into a fight, my parents only scolded me." Listening to these stories, it seems there aren't many people who actually recall having hurt others, but there are so many who feel that they have been hurt.

I met a woman who was deeply hurt because her mother had left home, abandoning her. She cried telling me how, decades later, she met her mother but still couldn't let go of feeling hurt. "My mother is already over seventy, but I still can't forgive her. Sometimes, I feel so tormented that I wonder if I should make peace with her, but I don't know how."

Her tears were not from the hurt of being abandoned by her mother, but from clinging to the hurt she felt when she was abandoned in the past. It was the memory of being abandoned that was making her sad, not the abandonment itself.

Most of our suffering is caused by our memories. We dwell on our misery by conjuring up memories of the times when we were disappointed or bullied by others. Yet we are the ones who expand and reproduce our pain, by preserving clear images of things that happened, and then clinging to those images. It's like locking ourselves in a dark cave.

Harboring bad memories of the past deep inside our minds and constantly brooding over them is like watching a movie. When we recall a past event, our brain mistakes the imagery we create for an event happening right now, in the present, in front of our eyes. When we recall something good, we involuntarily smile, and when we recall something painful and sad, we cry or feel heavy-hearted.

Our emotions arise unconsciously. If we preserve the emotional pain we experienced in the past, our current lives are likely to be miserable. These memories exist only in our minds; they have no tangible reality in the present moment. When we habitually recall the past, it's like we are repeatedly watching the same video clip over and over again. Many of us know people who only like to talk about "the good old days," as if they are still living in the past.

All our emotional wounds exist only in our minds, which hold onto these events and ideas as memories. We suffer, not because someone hurt us, but because we feel hurt over past events that may or may not have caused injury at the time. We harbor that hurt in our minds, and then dwell on our hurt feelings.

Do not carry the past on your shoulders like a crushing

burden. If you clearly understand that your present sadness originates from your own memories, healing your emotional wounds becomes simple. You can choose to break away from the past. Instead of dwelling on your sadness by continually replaying the memories in your head, you can redirect your attention to the here and now.

It may be true that your mother abandoned you, but she might have been in a situation that forced her to do so, a situation of which you were never aware. When you're little, you're easily hurt, so you might have resented your mother at the time. But now that you've grown up enough to become a mother yourself, you should try to understand that she had no choice but to abandon her own child. At that point, you might feel differently. You might even think to yourself: "Mom, thank you for giving birth to me. I am in this world thanks to you."

If you were to stop resenting her and start thanking her instead, you might gradually stop feeling gloomy and begin to brighten up. This might help you stop feeling like a victim who was abandoned and unloved.

Other than yourself, there's no one in the world who torments, hurts, or makes you feel anxious. You suffer because you harbor negative memories deep inside. Understanding this starts the healing process.

Everyone in this world can be happy. No matter how awful your experience was as a child, it's now in the past. If you stop replaying the videos in your head, you can choose to be happy at any moment. The present moment is the only moment in which you are actually alive and breathing. If you concentrate on the present, you will be free from suffering.

Furthermore, if you can concentrate on the present, all the things you experienced in the past may become valuable assets. Whether you failed in your business, broke up with your partner, or got hurt by someone, if you take all these life events as precious experiences that help you understand your life, they will enable you to deal wisely with whatever comes your way.

Regret Is Clinging onto
Past Mistakes

"If only I hadn't made that mistake. If only I had done that instead."

When people say these things, regretting their past actions, it may come across as self-reflection or introspection, but such words convey the message that the speaker is, at that moment, not happy.

Feelings of regret can involve the act of repenting past wrongdoing. But for the most part, regret is about tormenting ourselves by not being willing or able to forgive ourselves for the mistakes we've made. When we experience regret, we need to carefully observe our state of mind.

A woman told me that she regrets saying hurtful things to her mother: "My mother lives in the countryside all by herself. She often complains that her children don't understand her, and that it's no use raising children. I understand how she feels and am sorry, but when she blames us, I become resentful and feel like she's nagging again. A few days ago, I lost my temper when she complained, and since then, I haven't called her. I really regret it."

Many people experience conflict with their parents. The children who don't understand their parents eventually learn to understand them as they themselves age. When children are young and rebellious, they don't listen, no matter what their parents try to tell them. When they grow up and have children of their own, they realize how much heartache their parents must have experienced raising them.

Only when you get old and feeble yourself, when you end up living alone after losing your spouse, will you then be able to understand the loneliness of an aged, isolated mother. Even though you may not really be able to understand how old people feel, if you try to understand them and ease their loneliness, you may not feel as lonely when you yourself grow old. Therefore, you could take care of your own mother in order to prevent the suffering you might experience when you grow old, in addition to doing it for your mother's sake.

Parents who live a hard life in the countryside may think they will be taken care of by their children and live comfortably after retirement, since they worked hard and made sacrifices to raise their children. The surprising reality is often that when the children grow up, they are so busy making their own living that they hardly visit their parents.

Because parents feel lonely, they lament their fate. They grow disappointed with their children, and out of resentment, they may say things like, "How could my children be so uncaring, when we sacrificed so much to raise them?"

It's not difficult to solve this problem if you can think about what your parents went through to raise you. You need to think, "I'm sorry I don't visit you often enough."

If you repent in this way, you won't feel resentful even when your mother blames you. If your mother says she's disappointed in you, you can empathize with her and say, "You're right. It's no use raising children!" This will not only comfort your mother, but it will ease your own feelings as well.

If, however, you think to yourself, "There she goes again.

It's not like she's the only person who ever raised children," what your mother says will feel to you like nagging. You will resent her and feel irritated and frustrated. When you feel frustrated, you're likely to argue, which will make you even more reluctant to call, which will, in turn, leave you feeling regretful and sad.

If your mother were to suddenly die right after you have a falling out, you would no doubt be regretful and blame yourself for having been a terrible child to her. If you don't want to repeat such foolish behavior, you should care for your mother to the best of your ability. If your habit has been to call every week, try calling her twice a week. If you have visited twice a year, try to visit four times a year. If you presently visit every month, you should visit her twice each month.

You need to relieve her deep sorrow with twice the effort you were making before. Her sorrow is not just her own. When she passes away, it will become yours, and you will regretfully think, "I should have been nicer to her when she was alive." If you have such regret in your heart, you'll feel a deep sorrow. Being kind to your parents now will be good for you in the end.

It's foolish to regret and blame yourself for past wrongdoings. To regret is to hate yourself for making a mistake or for not having dealt with something properly. Regret is, in fact, a form of self-abuse. Your inability to forgive yourself for making mistakes usually stems from subconsciously thinking too highly of yourself, which makes you unwilling to accept that you can make mistakes. Usually, you regret your behavior because you think of yourself as an exceptional person.

Not being able to forgive others is hate; not being able to forgive yourself is regret. Regret is different from repentance. You regret it because you cling to the idea that you are an extraordinary human being. Regret happens when you berate yourself with the idea that such an outstanding person as yourself should not have done something so wrong or shouldn't have acted like a fool. If you can acknowledge and accept that you are not so outstanding that you never make mistakes, you will no longer feel regret.

If you regret something, you will dwell on it. Repentance happens when you realize that you made a mistake, resolve never to make the same foolish mistake again, and move on. If you fall down, crying serves no productive purpose.

You should just get up and try to make sure that you don't stumble in the same way again. The first step in repentance is being contrite about past wrongdoing, and the second is vowing never to do it again.

Humans are not particularly special. We make mistakes and do wrong. Instead of blaming yourself, tell yourself, "I have done wrong. I will not make the same mistake again," and then move on. Rather than regretting and blaming yourself, repent and move forward.

Anxiety Is the Result of an Obsession with the Future

In addition to making ourselves miserable by clinging to past events we can't change, we also worry and feel anxious about a future that has yet to arrive. Even though the future has not happened, people incessantly worry about and fear it.

"What if I fail the exam?"

"What if I get sick?"

"How should I spend my old age after raising my children?"

We can't seem to let go of our worries, not even for a moment. As if it's not enough to be tormented about a past that has already gone by, we are anxious and worried about things that have not yet, and may never, happen.

A single woman in her mid-thirties told me about her anxiety about the future: "Since I work freelance, I'm occasionally seized with anxiety and worry about my old age. Rather than my lack of a stable income, it's my lack of a clear plan or goal that causes these thoughts. When I was young, I always had goals I wanted to achieve and worked hard toward them. But at one point, it occurred to me that I didn't need to work so hard, so I quit my job. Right now, my mind is at ease, but I sometimes feel anxious and confused about whether it's all right to live day to day without a goal."

It seems contradictory that she feels confused when her mind is at ease. If she wants to live frantically on her job, she can do so. If she stops living such a hectic life because she thought it was a problem, she should lead a relaxed life.

The reason the young woman felt anxious and questioned whether it's all right to live without a goal is that, until that point, she had been working so hard toward her goals, and her habit of frantic goal-seeking had not yet been broken. Her habit remained in her subconscious, and now that she wasn't working so hard, she felt anxious about lagging behind others and wasting time. You become like a smoker trying to find better quality cigarettes rather than simply quitting the habit of smoking. Or maybe you feel like an alcoholic trying to get better liquor rather than trying to stop drinking.

Smoking is always worse than not smoking at all, no matter how high the quality of the cigarette. The same applies to drinking. You'll have nothing to worry about if you just let go of these habits and decide not to have them in your life. If you don't come to this realization, you'll falter whenever you run across what seems to be the best quality cigarettes or liquor.

When you see your friends drinking and smoking, you may ask yourself why you should be the only one excluded from such fun things. This feeling indicates that you still haven't been able to completely break away from your drinking and smoking habits. Even the highest quality liquor and cigarette means nothing to a person who doesn't drink or smoke. Likewise, if you understand that money or status are not the way to happiness, there will be no reason for you to feel anxious watching other people amassing money or getting promoted while you're making other choices.

We can find examples in the natural world. Is there some purpose or goal to Earth rotating around the sun? No, the Earth simply rotates in accordance with natural laws. On

Earth, plants germinate, grow, blossom, and die. Is there some purpose or plan behind this? What purpose do squirrels and rabbits have for running around so busily? What purpose do groundhogs have when they dig holes in the ground? They are all simply leading their lives as they were born to do.

Humans are born, live as a part of nature, and die, the same as a clump of grass or a rabbit. Living with no thought about the purpose of life neither diminishes human dignity nor destroys the order of nature. There is no reason to be anxious about not having any purpose in life.

Our lives are miserable because we think they should have a purpose. We are anxious, restless, and miserable because we give too much meaning to life. If you had breakfast this morning, what is there to be anxious about? If you have a warm place to sleep tonight, what is there to be anxious about?

The woman who came to me for advice chose to be a freelancer because she didn't want to be tied to a company, work for somebody else, or be bossed around. She wants to live as she pleases, sleep when she wants, travel when she feels like it, and write when she wants to write. In fact, it's not true that she has nothing she wants to do; the fact is that she has too many things she wants to do. Whatever she does, she wants to do everything her own way. There is no greater greed than this in the world.

She quit working for a company because she wanted to live as she wished. But then, she became anxious and restless because she was worried about the future, about what would happen in the future if she continued to live this way. Her attachment to the future makes her anxious in the present.

Perhaps 80% or 90% of anxiety comes from thoughts about the future. To ease this restlessness and anxiety about the future, we need to consider that today's troubles are enough for today. When I say this, people ask me how they can live thinking only about today. They assert that we must all think about tomorrow, the day after tomorrow, a year from now, ten years from now, and so on.

It's good to be prepared for the future, but if you think too much about it, you have the same subjective experience as when you actually encounter that for which you are preparing – your mind becomes anxious and restless. This becomes an illness of the mind.

Anxiety can affect one's physical health. A woman in her forties once told me that she felt something was wrong with her health, and that she couldn't sleep because she felt so anxious about it. "I felt a lump in my throat and had some tests," she told me. "I'm waiting for the results, and it's hard not to be anxious and restless. How should I control my mind?"

When you find that something is wrong with your body, your options are pretty simple. You can go to a medical professional and have your body examined. If you already had a test, you just need to wait for the results.

If the lump in her throat turns out to be a benign tumor, her reaction should be gratitude for the good news. Considering that it might have been a malignant tumor, she should feel extremely grateful.

Even if it did turn out to be cancer, isn't it fortunate that this too can be treated? If she had found out a year later, it would have been more difficult to treat. The doctor's job is to treat the cancer, so the woman can entrust her treatment to her doctor. She might worry about the possibility of dying during surgery, but that's not something she can know ahead of time. Worrying won't make the surgery more likely to succeed, and not worrying won't make it more likely to fail.

In a situation like this, you have two options: The first is to pray that everything will turn out fine. You may think, "I'm grateful that I'm able to have surgery. It's fortunate that this is operable." The second is to take the opportunity to practice letting go of your attachment to the body. You can think to yourself, "I thought I would live forever, but the body can collapse overnight! The body is not something to be attached to!"

With these realizations, you can live the rest of your life with a lighter heart. Whether it's about the preparation for a test, a life plan, or a health problem, anxiety comes from being fixated on the future. Instead of worrying about the future, pay attention to what is happening in the present. Tell yourself repeatedly that everything will be fine, whatever the result may be, and you will gradually see your anxiety disappear.

Most of the time, we are not aware of the present moment. When we spend our days thinking about the past or worrying about the future, we fail to be awake to the present. Happiness won't materialize on its own. When you focus on the present and do your best, these moments accumulate, and they become your happy future.

Superiority Complexes and Inferiority Complexes Come from the Same Place

We usually compare ourselves to others and make judgments about ourselves. If we judge that our circumstances are better than those of others, we feel superior. If our circumstances are worse, we feel inferior. There is no absolute standard against which to measure your position. Our judgment depends on who we compare ourselves to.

A man I knew felt insecure about his looks because he was teased when he was young. He told me: "My face is bigger than that of other people. I've been teased a lot because of it, which hurt me. As a result, I've been miserable and lonely for 37 years. I'm very sensitive and timid, so I have few friends.

I don't even sleep well because I'm so dissatisfied with my appearance. What should I do?"

I asked him a question and it resulted in the following dialogue:

"Is this bottle big or small?"

"It seems small."

"When you compare it with a table, is it big or small?"

"It's small."

"When you compare it with a watch, is it big or small?"

"It's big."

"Then, when you just look at this bottle by itself, is it big or small?"

"Isn't it about average?"

We make judgments about objects by comparing them with other things. We perceive an object as small in one moment, and at other times see it as large. When we say something is large or small, new or old, superior or inferior, old or young, long or short, we feel as if we are making objective evaluations. But these evaluations are highly subjective and are based on our own perceptions.

How you evaluate the size of any face will differ according to the size of the face you compare it to. There is no definite standard against which to measure which face is big and which is small. The size of the man's face wasn't the real problem. He just hadn't been able to heal the deep wound that was caused by the memory of other children telling him his face was too big.

When we look at ants in an ant hive, they appear to be identical. But if you were to take each ant and weigh it individually, their weight would all be different. The relative sizes of their heads, antennae, eyes, and abdomens would all be different as well.

So, which ant is the good-looking ant, and which one is ugly? If you used a microscope to examine the ants, you might find that their faces are all different, but I don't think any one of them suffers from an inferiority complex about its looks. A fact or circumstance becomes a problem only when you think it's a problem. Differences in appearance are just differences. They're not problems in and of themselves. People with a superiority complex and those with an inferiority complex both accept the standards of others in different aspects of their lives. Feeling superior or inferior is a psychological phenomenon that occurs when people compare their lives with the lives of others, instead of becoming the masters of their own lives. The feelings of superiority and inferiority have the same root.

Celebrities who look beautiful and talented to us tend to have greater inferiority complexes than ordinary people. That's because an inferiority complex comes from delusions about or high expectations of oneself.

"I look pretty good, but my eyes are too small."

"My face is fine, but my nose is ugly."

"My lips are fine, but my teeth look weird."

Oddly enough, celebrities are more insecure about their appearances than ordinary people. After all, an inferiority complex is not caused by being unable to meet some absolute standard, but by being unable to meet one's own expectations.

There are no inferior or superior beings in this world. All beings are simply different. If we were to pick twenty ordinary people and rate everything about them – their height, weight, size of eyes and nose, length of arms and fingers, running ability, long jump ability, cooking ability, and so forth – we could evaluate them based upon various rankings. If we rank each person using only one trait, each member of the group would seem very different from the others. But if we rated 1,000 characteristics of those twenty people, their total scores would be pretty similar because even though everyone is different, overall, people are similar.

During certain historical periods, situations, or circumstances, only a few factors were used to rank people. During the Joseon Dynasty in Korea, the civil service examination ranked only literary ability. Yet in the current modern society, people with singing or dancing abilities are highly admired. If you were born 100 years ago, your ability to pitch a ball well would have been useless, but in this time period you could potentially earn a lot of money as a baseball player. Even the most coveted ability will change according to the time period and the values prevalent in that period.

To be free from an inferiority complex, you need to recognize it's a delusion. Even a physical disability is not an inferiority, but rather an inconvenience. For instance, if you can view not having one arm as merely inconvenient, you can overcome that inconvenience by learning to compensate or getting an artificial limb.

The first step to overcoming a superiority or inferiority complex and becoming happy is to view the given situation in a positive manner. You may base this on the knowledge that all beings are simply different. A Buddhist monk, for example, should think of himself as a person who lives without a partner. If I compared myself to married people, I would feel inferior. This may also mean that I can't be satisfied with my life as a monk. But on the other hand, if I had not become a monk, I wouldn't have been able to give Dharma talks as freely as I do now. There are so many things I can do because I live the way I do.

When you feel bad about yourself, you may think, "I'm neither this nor that. What am I?" Try to change your thoughts to "I am this, and I am that also." When you view your circumstances in a positive manner, things will work out for the better, and you can become more confident in your life.

Feelings
Arise, Stay, Change, and Disappear

The body is composed of a combination of physical elements, and it changes according to its current state of health. Old cells die and new cells replace them. We think our bodies remain the same, but they're constantly changing as they go through the process of birth and death. Such changes are called "birth, aging, sickness, and death."

It's the same with the mind. When an emotion arises, we may feel like it will last, but it soon scatters and disappears. This is called "arising, staying, changing, and disappearing."

We want other people to stay the same, but that's an impossible expectation. Even though you promise "to love until death do us part," your feelings will change over time. That is one of the characteristics of the mind. You suffer when you are unaware of such characteristics and want other people to stay the same.

Feelings continuously arise and disappear from moment to moment; they have no substance in either shape or form. Still, we become worried and anxious as we cling to feelings of happiness, sadness, or loneliness that arise in the moment.

A woman came to me for advice, worried that her boyfriend's feelings toward her would change after marriage: "I don't think it's bad to fall out of love while you're dating," she said, "but as I began thinking more seriously about getting married, I became worried about him falling out of love with me after marriage. I believe that after you get married, you can't simply replace your spouse when your feelings toward him or her change; you have to stay married to that person for the rest of your life. Since I began thinking this way, my love life hasn't been going well. Maybe it's because my mind is burdened with this thought. Is there any way for feelings not to change or to change for the better?"

There is no such way. The mind cannot remain constant. One moment you like someone; the next moment you hate them. One moment you and your partner seem like a match made in heaven, and the next you seem like sworn enemies. The mind keeps changing. That's the nature of the mind, and it cannot be judged as right or wrong.

There is a saying, "Once on shore, we pray no more." We feel differently when we borrow money from a friend, compared to when we have to pay it back. Also, we feel different about our partner when we are dating compared to when we are married.

Once you're married, you may become attracted to someone else and want to date them. Rather than denying such feelings, you need to simply refuse to act on them. If you knew there would be negative consequences when you acted on your desire, you wouldn't do it. Likewise, if you knew that you would suffer a loss if you didn't do something, you'd go ahead and do it.

When you are dating someone, it's not a big deal to break up because the relationship isn't legally binding. If your partner no longer loves you or you become weary of your partner, it's better to break up. You will suffer less by ending the relationship. If, after getting married, you continue to follow your desires, there will be negative consequences.

For that reason, you need to move beyond your momentary impulses rather than act on them.

Marriage doesn't guarantee that your feelings will remain constant. In fact, it's impossible to have positive feelings toward your spouse all the time. When negative emotions arise, rather than being swayed by them, you have the option of viewing your life with a long-term perspective: "Essentially, emotions arise and then disappear." If you're aware of this, you can avoid any damage that could result from being controlled by your emotions.

The path to happiness doesn't depend on feelings remaining constant, but in knowing that feelings inevitably change and that you don't have to act on them. Realizing this, you can have a peaceful life since you will be neither overly excited when you like something nor too depressed when something displeases you.

No matter how strongly we demand that someone remains utterly steadfast in the way they feel, this is still an impossibility. All we can do is accept that people's feelings change. In the case of married life, you must choose whether or not to stay with your spouse despite your changed feelings.

Feelings arise, stay for a while, change, and then disappear.

The process may differ in terms of detail from one relationship to another, but the experience is common to everyone. We mistakenly believe that feelings won't change, so as a result, we suffer. If you know how the mind works, you can be free of the suffering that comes from vainly trying to change others or from hating others for not changing the way you want them to.

Formed Habits
Can Be Changed

For a pine tree to take root in a crevice between rocks on a cliff and survive, there must be constant interaction between the tree and its environment. Humans are the same. Our habits and behaviors take root over time through our interactions with our environment.

Our personality is made up of habits, and they don't change easily because they are a form of unconscious inertia. However, we often want to change our habits quickly, and this may cause us to fail. As a result, we tend to blame ourselves and think, "I am the problem." Likewise, we get annoyed and angry when others can't change their personalities right away.

We often become impatient about our habits not changing quickly. We respond by getting angry, hating others, or feeling discouraged. As habits are so deeply rooted in our subconscious and are so hard to change, people say we are destined to be that way. However, all habits have been acquired, and because nothing is permanent, habits can be changed though this requires a lot of effort.

If you want to quit smoking, a conflict will arise between your conscious desire to stop and your habitual, behavioral pattern developed at the subconscious level. The inertia of ingrained smoking habits conflicts with the new desire for change.

Our mind arises from the subconscious, whereas willpower is part of our conscious mind. When consciousness tries to control the subconscious, it fails most of the time. There is an old saying, "Resolutions don't last more than three days." Trying to control the subconscious with conscious intentions rarely works. As a result, we are sometimes tempted to do things we know we shouldn't do, either ethically or morally. We say that we know what we should do and shouldn't do, but our actions don't follow our intentions.

Words and actions are more influenced by the subconscious mind than by conscious thought or will. During exam time, students know they should study, but they may become tired and doze off because their instinct to relieve fatigue by falling asleep is stronger than their will to study.

Consider a student who is preparing for a test. She asks her mom to wake her up at 3 AM. Then, just to be on the safe side, she also sets the alarm and goes to sleep. When her mother wakes her up and the alarm rings, she opens her eyes briefly, but then goes back to sleep. In the morning, she complains that her mother didn't wake her up. But, if, instead of taking an exam, she was going on a picnic, she would have woken up earlier without even needing an alarm or a wake-up call.

This is the difference between conscious and subconscious behavior. Deciding to wake up at a certain hour is an act of consciousness. But when you're asleep, you are in a subconscious state. Waking up earlier than usual because of a dream, or in anticipation of an exciting event, is an act of subconscious guidance. Most often, only the things that you like a great deal, or that move you deeply, can influence the subconscious.

You might make a conscious decision that feels to you like a firm resolution, but it won't last unless it's accepted by your subconscious. Even though your conscious thoughts have changed, your behavior won't change unless your subconscious changes too. The reason it's difficult to overcome your weakness, even when others keep reminding you about it and you make sincere efforts to change, is that your will to overcome it isn't able to override the resistance posed by the inertia of your subconscious.

It's not easy to change unconscious behavior, but it's not impossible. If you have a strong will, you can even change your karma although it seems impossible to change. Before expecting any change to occur, however, you need to know that karma does not change easily.

Start to work on changing your karma with the awareness that there will be many trials and errors, and that it will take a long time. Sometimes a strong impact, like an electric shock, can bring about an abrupt change, but such cases are rare.

To change the habits that determine our fate requires steady effort and a strong will. The problem is that most people don't make steady effort, or they don't have a sufficiently strong will. They try for a little while and then give up. Perhaps they wonder why they should bother to change, and they may believe that they can go on living without changing their behavior after all.

You need to believe that you can change and sustain your efforts over time. If you persevere, new habits will form and come to reside in your subconscious. As your habits change, so will your fate.

PART 03

HOW TO LIVE
WITH PEOPLE WHO HAVE
DIFFERENT OPINIONS
FROM YOURS

When we meet people, a certain mentality is at work. As we meet them for the first time, we start out with the premise that they are different from us. So, we put up our guard and probe into them. If we find something in common, in terms of perspective, place of birth, or name, we are happy and befriend them quickly. We become friends, lovers, or colleagues. Once we become close with them, the premise, "We are different" changes to "We are the same." As a result, our relationship appears to have become stronger.

However, this is when conflicts begin. We thought they were the same as us, but we find that they are different. We discover that they're different in terms of personality, view, and palate. The fact is they haven't changed. We thought they were the same as us and were compatible with us based on our limited knowledge about them. Then, we get into conflict with them because we think they are doing something unexpected or something extremely wrong.

All Conflicts Stem from Relationships

In the course of our lives, we meet with and part from a countless number of people. When we meet someone we like, there's no problem. There's also no problem when we part from someone we don't like. However, we feel miserable when we have to part from someone who we are fond of or when we have to meet with someone we don't like.

The Buddha referred to suffering in life as the "84,000 afflictions" in the sense that humans experience countless afflictions. These afflictions are also referred to as the "108 afflictions" or "eight sufferings." The eight sufferings include "the suffering of having to part from those you love" and "the suffering of having to meet with those you hate."

Again, you suffer if the situation calls for you to separate from someone you love, and you also suffer if the situation calls for you to be with someone you hate.

Tolerating a spouse you dislike because you can't easily get a divorce is suffering. Alternately, you might love your husband and suffer because of having to live with a mother-in-law you dislike. Even though you like your job and get paid well, working with a boss or coworker you dislike is suffering. When you dislike something, whether it's a marriage or a job, you would be fine if you could just quit. But if, for whatever reason, you can't quit, you'll suffer.

It's natural to think that because suffering is usually caused by relationships, the problem will be solved if we sever the relationship. Thus, we refuse to meet with those we don't like, get divorced from a spouse, or leave home if we don't get along with a family member. But rather than making us happy, these actions are likely to make us feel lonelier and even more miserable. Suffering arises when we begin a relationship, as well as when we end one. When the relationship we formed in order to be happy causes suffering, the reason lies not in the relationship itself, but in having formed the relationship in an erroneous manner.

Many people ask me questions about how to form romantic relationships, how to get married, how to raise a child, how to take care of their parents, and how to deal with their work life. All these questions appear different on the surface, but when we examine them closely, they're all based on relationship issues. Each relationship appears to be slightly different according to the conditions under which it was formed, but the principle at work is similar.

Conflicts arising from relationships all start from the fact that everyone is different. We tend to become disappointed and distressed because our personalities, religions, preferences, hometowns, or habits are different from those of others.

Let's take a look at people's appearances. Are they the same or different? People have some common features, but there are often many differences. We all have two eyes, one nose, and one mouth, but upon closer examination, these features have different shapes and sizes. The same applies to people's thoughts. Everybody thinks differently, but the closer we are to someone, the more we want them to have the same thoughts and feelings as we do. We become disappointed with others for not being like-minded and resent them for not doing what we want them to do.

When you pick up a handful of soybeans and examine them closely, their size, color, and shape are all slightly different. At first glance, they may look the same, but when you look at them closely, they're different. But what about when you compare them with red beans? In comparison to how markedly different soybeans are from red beans, the slight differences among the soybeans become insignificant. Individual soybeans may differ in size, shape, and color, but when we compare them to red beans, they're all identifiable as soybeans. When the soybeans are compared to one another, they are different, but when compared with red beans, they are all soybeans.

The things we encounter every day have dual characteristics; they have both similarities to and differences from other things. Even when they're different in some respects, they are the same in others. When they're the same in some respects, they are different in others. Likewise, beings are neither the same nor different. When we say things are different or the same, the difference or the similarity lies not in the things themselves but in our perception of them. Beyond our perception, beings are just beings.

When conflict arises in a relationship because of a difference of opinion, there are two ways to resolve it. The first is to accept each other's differences, saying, "I think this way, and you think that way." This doesn't mean that I'm right, and you're wrong or that you're right, and I'm wrong. It's simply accepting that we are all different. Accepting someone who is different from us is equal to respecting that person. To respect the other person is to accept that person as they are, instead of judging them as right or wrong.

The second way to resolve a conflict in a relationship is to understand the other person: "From that person's point of view, they would think that way." "From my child's position, they would behave that way." "From my husband's position, he could take it that way." "From my wife's position, she'd react that way." "From the viewpoint of the Japanese, it's possible to come to that conclusion." "From the viewpoint of the North Koreans, they could take such measures." To think this way is to understand others.

Accepting and understanding that the other person is different from you is the most fundamental mindset to have when forming relationships. If you can remember these two perspectives when forming a relationship, you will be able to prevent the majority of conflicts.

A Good Person Versus
a Bad Person

Everyone wants to have good relationships with good people. But what kind of person is a good person? How can we distinguish between a good person and a bad person?

A college student once asked me: "As I get older, I'm meeting a lot of different people. What do I need to do to form relationships with good people?"

So, I asked her in return. "Are you a good person?"

She replied, "I think I'm a good person."

"Everybody considers themselves a good person, so it's hard to tell who is actually a good person. How, then, should we distinguish between a good person and a bad person?"

"Shouldn't we start by distinguishing the factors that make a person bad?"

"But what is bad? Let's say a woman has been a good Catholic for more than 30 years but suddenly converts to Protestantism or Buddhism. What would the members of her Catholic church think?"

"I guess they would think she is bad."

"What about Protestants or Buddhists?"

"I guess they would think she is great?"

"They'd probably say she has finally come to her senses. In such a case, how is it possible to distinguish between being a good person and a bad person? Let's say you have a boyfriend, but you think he's not such a good person and break up with him. Will he remain single for the rest of his life, or will he meet other women?"

"I guess he'll meet other women."

"After you break up with him, he will likely meet other women. If your boyfriend thinks you're not such a good person and breaks up with you, you will very likely meet other men. In this case, what is good and what is bad?"

"It depends on your viewpoint."

"That's right. You said you wanted to meet a good person,

so what will you do?"

"Choose a person who is good based on my perspective."

"Do you think that your perspective will be the same as those of your parents, or different?

"It will probably be different. But I think I'll like the person I have chosen because I perceive him to be good."

The person you like is a good person to you. If someone else thinks that same person is bad, then this is a bad person for that person. Any person appears to be good or bad according to the karma of the one evaluating them. However, the fact is they are neither absolutely good nor absolutely bad.

When they perceive others as good or bad, each person has a different framework of perception. Protestants and Buddhists have different frameworks of perception, just as if they were wearing glasses with different colored lenses. From a historical perspective, Koreans and Japanese have different frameworks of perception. Koreans think of Ahn Jung-geun as a patriot who fought for Korea's independence. In the eyes of the Japanese, he was a terrorist.

Consider a man who worked hard and saved money for his old age. His wife, a devoted Buddhist, donates $100,000 to a temple without his knowledge. Those at the temple will think that the wife is a great person, but her family will most likely come to the conclusion that she is out of her mind. The same exact action can provoke opposite reactions in people, depending on their positions and views.

The standard we use when we describe someone as "good" is really how well that person treats us. Those who are good to us can be divided into two categories: The first category consists of people who benefit us materially or emotionally. The second category consists of people who agree with us. Generally, people we don't like are those who do the opposite.

All our efforts to distinguish between good people and bad people come from seeing the errors in our perception as objective realities. We say, "You are bad," when the truth is, we should say instead, "You bother me." We mistakenly think of another person as being objectively bad when, in fact, it's simply a matter of us feeling that the other person is bad.

You will always encounter people you like and people you don't like. If you form relationships only with those you like, you won't get to know as many people. If you insist on following your preferences, you'll neither want to nor be able to find out the true value of interacting with different people. Instead, you'll be quite limited in the range of people you meet and get to know.

You need to meet many different people in order to know and understand that there are all kinds of people. If you want to meet good people, you must first open your heart to all. If you can do this, you'll be able to meet and learn about people of all kinds. As a result, you will be able to get along with a wide range of people.

No One Has Everything
in This World

There are some people who have never been in romantic relationships, but the reason isn't that they are somehow lacking. When people with little dating experience talk to me about their love life, they usually say something like the following: "I'm at least average-looking, my personality isn't too bad, and my job is okay. So, why haven't I been able to have a romantic relationship? Why can't I get married?"

The reason might be that their standards are too high. If our standards are unreasonably high, approaching someone who meets those standards will be intimidating. It's easy to approach someone that we don't think too highly of. It's much more difficult to approach someone who meets our highest standards. There's a bigger chance that they'll reject us, and their rejection will be more painful. This is similar to how we become tense when we're around someone in a high social position or someone who is rich or famous. We want to get acquainted with them, but we feel tense or fearful about the outcome.

Another thing those people often say is, "There aren't many attractive people around, and all the good ones are already taken." If you find only those who are already committed to other relationships attractive, this means that you have unreasonably high standards. Let's use work as an analogy. Many people want to work for a large firm or work as a lawyer or a doctor because those jobs are considered prestigious. Many competent and talented people covet such jobs or only want to work in settings that offer excellent work conditions. As a result, such jobs become difficult or impossible to find. In the same way, you may consider your standards to be quite reasonable when looking for a prospective date, but your standards might be unrealistically high.

Another reason might be that your parents didn't get along

when you were young. When marital life is full of conflict, people regret their marriage, and they say to their children, "Gosh, your father/mother drives me crazy." They complain about their spouses in front of their children, regardless of whether or not the children have the capacity to understand what's happening. Inevitably, the children develop negative feelings about their parents. Then, when they grow up and enter into their own romantic relationships, they tend to have underlying feelings of anxiety about marriage. At a critical moment in a relationship, they tend to run away. If you find marriage burdensome, the sentiment is likely related to something you experienced as a child that remains in your subconscious.

The third reason might be a bad experience the person had as a child, such as sexual abuse by an adult. Even though they forgot about the incident, such negative experiences could make them fear or reject marriage.

The last reason might be that they saw their friends become miserable and resentful after breaking up with their love interests. This might make them think to themselves, "I should be very careful about whom I date."

Someone you initially thought was nice might turn out

to be otherwise after dating for a while. Therefore, it's not necessarily bad to date someone and end up breaking up with them.

Looking at these possible reasons, you first need to uncover the reason that you're not able to have a romantic relationship. When you know the reason, you will be able to solve the problem and open your heart.

When you look for a person with whom to have a romantic relationship or when you get married, you become very selective. You can't date or marry just anyone, so you try to choose carefully. It's understandable, but if you want someone of the right age, academic background, money, and so on, it will be very hard to find a person who seems just right. Thus, it's very difficult to get married.

In the old days, there were drug peddlers at rural markets who sold medicine while handling snakes. They used to say, "If you take this medicine, you will be cured of all illnesses." They would hawk their medicines loudly and enthusiastically in the markets, and people would gather around. Obviously, there is no such panacea in the current world, but blinded and deafened by greed, people are seduced by the idea of a cure-all.

Relationships can work the same way. As is the case with

objects, no one person has everything. A sharp knife is useful for working in the kitchen, but it could cause bodily harm if used in the wrong way. Cotton is soft, but it has no strength. Everything in this world has such a duality.

Yet we want our prospective mates to possess every single desirable quality, such as intelligence, gentleness, kindness, and leadership. This is impossible. We want our spouses to be perfect and to excel in every way.

We develop certain expectations: "Our next-door neighbor's husband does a lot of their housework. Why can't you be like him?" "Our next-door neighbor's wife is good at housekeeping. Why can't you be like her?" When we criticize our spouses in this way, it's just like choosing cotton for its softness and then complaining about its lack of strength. Or it's like choosing a knife for its sharpness and then complaining about it having no softness.

There is no perfect person in the world. It would be better for you to think, "Well, no one has everything. The world is fair," rather than getting annoyed at your spouse for not meeting all your expectations.

No matter how carefully you look around the mountain, you can't find a tree that can be cut and used as a pillar as it is. However strong and beautiful the tree may be, it must be trimmed and polished before being used. By the same token, if you're ready to adapt to others and get along with them, you can get married with anyone. If you look for someone who will sweep you off your feet and fulfill your every need, you'll have a hard time finding someone to marry even if you search every corner of the world.

Moreover, you only truly get to know someone after spending time with them and living with them. A woman may appreciate a man for his decisiveness, but after living with him, she may find him to be stubborn, inconsiderate, and set in his ways. Another may marry a man because he is sweet and easy to get along with, but after living with him, she may find him frustratingly indecisive. The qualities that seemed wonderful when dating might become unbearable as time passes and this may cause couples to break up.

If you're not good at dating, it's better to start by making acquaintances. When the number of acquaintances you are comfortable with increases to 10, 20, and then 100, there might be someone for whom you have special feelings. If you meet people without requiring that they meet certain conditions, you might find someone compatible, even among older, younger, or divorced people.

If you go out to meet people with the goal of getting married, there will be few people you can date after excluding those who are divorced, too old, too young, or otherwise "imperfect." Moreover, as the person you're interested in also has to return your affections, it could turn out to be quite impossible to find someone to date at all.

Therefore, don't try to date only attractive women or men from the start. Tell yourself, "Anyone will do. I will try dating casually with about five people, and then maybe get into a serious relationship with the sixth."

It's good to date people with such a relaxed mindset. It's better to break up while dating than divorcing them after getting married. It's better to get a divorce when you don't have children than when you do.

Breaking up is not necessarily a bad thing. If you meet someone and get married without ever having dated anyone else, you'll miss all the opportunities to meet other people. It may be better for everyone if they date many different people before committing to marriage. However, if you date more than one person at a time, you may be criticized for being unfaithful. If your partner breaks up with you, it's not necessarily a bad thing. Then, you'll be able to date other people without being criticized.

It's wonderful when you and your partner love each other and succeed in getting married. However, you don't need to get hurt just because someone leaves you, since this may give you the chance to find someone more suitable.

You don't need to be afraid that your boyfriend or girlfriend might leave you. Your breaking up with them isn't a problem, either. These days, countless couples divorce, so breaking up with someone is no reflection on you.

After having dated three or more people, you will be able to understand people better. If you like your partner too much, they might feel burdened. If you are too standoffish, they might leave you. The right approach doesn't come through planning. You have to arrive at it through multiple experiences. This is called the learning effect, and you can get the hang of it through trial and error.

As you practice how to deal with people by dating a wide variety of partners, you will have fewer conflicts in your marriage.

Conditions for
a Happy Marriage

People say that, these days, it costs a fortune and requires a lot of preparation to get married. So, when choosing a prospective spouse, they carefully consider their partner's wealth and occupation. But are these conditions enough for a happy marriage?

A young man once asked me about the conditions for a happy marriage: "I've always had a vague idea that if two people have the same values and goals, they will be able to have a happy marriage. But as I get older, people give me advice such as, 'A man should have a certain amount in savings' or 'You should be able to afford an apartment or a house in the metropolitan area.' I can't ignore these practical conditions anymore. What kind of values should I have in order to have a happy marriage?"

There are two major conditions for marriage. First, you must be over 18 years old. In other words, you have to be physically grown up. Second, you should be independent from your parents and be willing to give up half of your rights to accommodate your spouse. Are you ready to adjust to your spouse? What if you want to go to the beach for your vacation, but your spouse wants to go to the mountains? Are you able to accommodate their wishes instead of insisting on what you want?

For two people who have different constitutions, thoughts, and ways of life to have a happy marriage, they should each be ready to give up half of their rights. Otherwise, no matter how grand their wedding, no matter how big their house, it will be difficult for the marriage to last. If you marry thinking, "They'll follow my wishes as they did when we were dating," without giving up any of your own rights, you're bound to run into conflicts.

Conflicts begin with trivial things. One partner puts away clothes neatly in the closet, but the other leaves them everywhere around the house. One thinks the food is too bland, but the other thinks it's seasoned just right. One thinks the room is hot and wants the air conditioner turned on, but the other thinks it's too cold and wants it turned off. One partner thinks it's necessary to shower daily, while the other disagrees. All these differences between partners will lead to conflicts and fights. Trivial things like these make marriage difficult. In reality, the size of your apartment or your car is not as important.

Many people considering marriage weigh only these secondary things, without mentally preparing to adjust to their spouses. Many marriages fail despite the abundant household appliances and other material goods that couples purchase for their lives together. In some cases, these couples break up while preparing for the wedding or divorce right after the honeymoon.

The marriage system was formed naturally over the course of the development of human civilization because it was beneficial to both parties in the marriage. In general, the development of human civilization follows the path of maximum efficiency. If you and your fiancé each have a room but decide to live together, you'll save rent on one of the rooms and on the cost of household goods. So, in that regard, the marriage will benefit both of you. When you lived alone, you had to perform household chores by yourself, but when you get married, you can share the burden, which will allow you to have more free time. This allocation of roles directly benefits both partners.

But remember, living together for mutual benefit means that you need to follow the wishes of your spouse. Let's say the wife wants her husband to prioritize spending time together over making a lot of money. Then, instead of saying, "Why do you complain so much when I earn a good living for you?" the husband should try to accommodate her wishes.

When you get married, you get the title of wife or husband, along with many new responsibilities. Partners in a marriage need to accommodate each other's wishes. You don't need to strain yourself to fulfill your role as husband or wife, but you need to do the best you can to become a good partner.

When you're dating, physical attraction may be the most important factor. But if you want to have a long and happy marriage, you need to find someone willing to adjust to you and someone who will benefit you as you benefit them. For example, as marriage is communal living, you should be ready to do your share of cooking, cleaning, and other household chores.

And, of course, an important condition for any marriage is the willingness to do your best to get along with your spouse. This is the most important condition for maintaining a happy marriage.

Are You Living a Good Life or a Life That Looks Good to Others?

Many young adults find themselves having to make sacrifices due to increased financial pressures and unemployment. It seems natural that if someone manages to find solid employment, they would not only be happy but would also be congratulated by many people.

A young woman once complained to me that she was miserable in a job she had landed four months prior but couldn't quit because it was a position at a prestigious firm: "When I'm getting ready to go to work in the morning, I feel so distressed that I'm almost always on the verge of tears. I often cry at work, and by the time I come home,

I'm heavyhearted and feeling sorry for myself. I want to quit my job. However, people around me tell me to stick it out since it will be very difficult for me to get a job at another prestigious firm, and because it's a great long-term job for a woman. But I feel so miserable every day, and I don't know what to do."

Let's imagine a smoker says to a non-smoking friend, "This is an excellent cigarette. Try it." The non-smoker tries it and finds that it hurts his throat and makes his eyes water. He doesn't feel like smoking anymore, but because his friend, the smoker, insists that the cigarette is first-class, he tries again. He continues to smoke through coughing fits and watery eyes. If smoking doesn't suit him, he can simply stop, but he's afraid to miss out on what he has been told is an excellent cigarette. So, he continues to smoke while complaining about the stinging throat. What a fool he is.

This is the same as hesitating to quit your job because others envy it and urge you not to quit. There is a saying that goes, "No matter how highly-regarded the governor's position is, if you don't want it, that's that." No matter how much others may commend and admire the job, if you hate it, it's not a good job for you. If you are miserable, you can simply quit. It's your life, so why should you care what others think? Go to work, bid your farewell, and hand in your resignation.

If you can't bring yourself to quit your job, you need to think about the reasons for your hesitation. If the reason is money, you can always make money in other ways, such as working as a housekeeper or maybe finding an online job. If that seems too hard, how about getting a janitorial position? If that also seems hard, consider other jobs.

Review a list of prospective jobs one by one. If you conclude that staying at your current job is the best option, that's great. If your position is stable and pays well, how can you expect to work without experiencing some difficulties? If you think, "I don't want this job no matter how high the salary," there's no need to hold on to it.

The fact that the young woman shed tears while asking me this question means that she felt the job was too good to quit but too stressful to keep. If you find yourself in this same situation, the root cause of your suffering is conflicted desire, so you need to let it go.

You can just hand in your resignation, but if you can't afford to do so, try comparing your job with other types of work that are much harder to do. Tell yourself, "I would only earn minimum wage doing manual labor, but my salary at my current job is twice that much" and go to work in good spirits.

If you're struggling at work even though you managed to land a job that others are envious of, it may be that your abilities were overestimated. If your competency were underestimated, you may feel a little disappointed. But that would be the end of it. If, however, your abilities are assessed too high to begin with, you may initially feel happy about receiving approval, but you'll soon feel a lot of stress. In order to meet those high expectations, you will have to work extremely hard.

If your competency has been overrated at work, you'll also feel anxious about letting others down. Inevitably, you will always be nervous and fearful that your incompetence might be exposed. In the worst case scenario, this could lead to a mental breakdown.

If your true ability level is 100%, it's best to represent yourself as having an ability of 80% at most. This is the way to live your life with ease.

If you were to have the ability level of 100% but were

thought to have the ability of only 50%, not many of your employers would criticize you, since they wouldn't expect very much. Over time, as they discover that you perform much better than expected, they would begin to respect you, and you would gain recognition from those around you.

On the other hand, what happens if you were to have an ability level of 50% but are thought to have the ability of 90% or 100%? When people begin working with you, they would find that your performance doesn't meet their original expectations, and they'd end up writing you off as incompetent. In such a case, your boss would become disappointed, and you would either end up being relegated to a trivial position or turning in your resignation. Obviously, it's wise not to overstate your abilities.

To avoid being stressed by having your abilities evaluated at work, perform at your actual level of aptitude, instead of going to great lengths to do well or trying too hard to impress others. Accept the situation as it is. Doing the work is your job, but evaluating your work is the job of management. There's an old Korean saying that goes, "People do the work, and the heavens do the rest." This means that you should do your best without obsessing about the results.

Even if you are able to think this way, it's not easy to change your long-standing habit of seeking praise. The greater the desire to perform well, the greater the disappointment when you don't get approval. Try to let go of the desire to do well, and just keep at your work with a light heart. Then, you will gradually see an improvement in your abilities.

The Boss Who Teaches You
the Middle Way

Imagine how much people would enjoy their jobs if the coworkers who spend a significant portion of their days together could be more understanding of each other and get along amicably. Most people say that the hardest part of their job is interpersonal relationships rather than the actual work itself.

A woman I met who works as a nurse said she found it extremely difficult to satisfy her boss's demands: "When my boss distributes work to the staff, she assigns five patients to me while assigning only four to the other nurses. When I sit down to work on the computer, she badgers me to get up and move quickly. When I move quickly to do as she demands, she changes her mind and says, 'You're moving too fast and making others feel nervous. You need to calm down.' I'm trying my best to adjust to her work style, but it's very difficult."

When experiencing this conflict at work, she has two choices. She can choose not to work with someone like her boss and leave the job. However, if she can't quit, she needs to accept the situation as it is.

If we compare this situation to something like farming, imagine this. A farmer might think that the seed he's planting is good, but the field is in poor condition. In that case, the farmer would have to plow the soil or plant the seed elsewhere. If the farmer can't afford to move to a new field, or if he has some compelling reason to remain in the original field, the only option is to adjust to the current conditions of that field.

This won't be easy, but each of us must be willing to endure some hardships in order to make a living. Imagine you're going up a mountain to collect some firewood. You might complain that the mountain is too high to climb, that the saw is too dull, or that the tree you found is too thick to cut down, which would leave you no choice but to go down the mountain without any wood.

If the nurse wants to be happy where she is without leaving the hospital, she must change her perspective. Her boss gave her more work compared to others, giving her five patients while only giving others four, but this is actually a good thing. She is doing a good deed based on her competence. Since she is working anyways, it's likely better that she can take care of five patients rather than idling after taking care of only four.

If her boss asks, "What are you doing?" when she's working on the computer, she should simply respond, "I'm typing in data." If her boss says, "You're moving too fast and are making others feel nervous. You need to calm down," she can respond by just slowing down a little. If the boss says, "too fast," slow down; when she says, "too slow," speed up a little. As she repeats this process, she will eventually find out the speed her boss prefers. This is important.

A nurse is paid for taking care of patients, and they accumulate blessings in the process. This is something to be thankful for. When her boss criticizes her for moving too fast, she should try to think, "She is helping me learn the

Middle Way." The Middle Way is adjusting oneself to what another person thinks is appropriate. Doing this does not make her spineless or lazy. Rather, it's doing the best she can under the given circumstances.

Again, the nurse's job is to take care of patients. People believe that nurses only need to care for patients, just as all teachers need only to teach their students diligently, but things are not so simple. Every organization has a manager, and it's important to get along with your boss if you want a pleasant work environment. So long as such a system is in place, you must be able to cater to your boss's disposition in addition to doing your job well.

This does not mean that you must flatter your bosses or walk on eggshells around them. Just see your boss as one of the people toward whom you should be considerate. If your boss makes unreasonable demands, such as telling you not to take care of patients, to administer the wrong medication, and so forth, you should flatly refuse. Otherwise, as a coworker, you should learn to accommodate their wishes. If you can work amicably with such a demanding boss, you won't have any problems even if you eventually take another job elsewhere.

Think of your current job as a training opportunity to develop the ability to accommodate all types of people. If you find it impossible to work with your current boss, you can always quit and find a different job. If, however, you are treated unfairly according to the law, you should not simply quit. In such a case, you must exercise your legal rights as a citizen and an employee.

Most Relationships Are Based on Selfishness

Most human beings are self-centered, and people want to form relationships that benefit them. When we seek to form and maintain a special relationship with someone, we have selfish motives, whether we're aware of them or not.

The same is true when choosing a prospective spouse. People select the person who will benefit them the most, taking into account various factors such as a person's finances, education, physique, and personality. Even parent-child relationships are based on selfishness, albeit to varying degrees. Children feel affection for their parents, not just because they gave birth to them and raised them, but because their parents are their principal benefactors.

As such, even if things seem fine at first, latent selfishness in human relationships will lead to conflicts over time. When dating someone, you may accept some small losses in the hopes of big gains in the future. This is like making a long-term investment.

Imagine you get married to someone after dating for a while. Six months into the marriage, your true feelings begin to emerge. You feel like you're not benefiting from the marriage as much as you had expected, so you may end up feeling that you are actually taking a loss. Eventually, you come to the conclusion that you'd be better off living alone.

I'm not saying that being self-centered in your relationships is necessarily harmful, but you need to be aware that others are likewise motivated by selfish interests when forming relationships. If you can understand that others, like you, also calculate gains and losses in forming interpersonal relationships, you won't think badly of a self-centered person, and you'll experience few interpersonal conflicts.

Imagine that your intention in some transaction was to give 3 items and receive 7. Chances are, the other person will have the same intent for themselves. When each of you only receive 3, naturally you'll be disappointed in each other. Your dissatisfaction and disappointment are not caused by the other person but by your expectations of receiving all 7 of those items.

A college student once consulted me on how to get along with an older student who only treated her well when she needed something from her. The younger student considered this to be a detestable trait: "There is a senior student who is the best student in our department. She's quite demanding and calculating. She is only nice to those she can control. For example, in class, several of us, including the two of us, sit in the same row, but she only shares her snack with people right next to her. I don't even like snacks, but it feels unpleasant to be left out. It annoys me that she is nice to me only when she needs something from me."

If this student who consulted me marries someone and maintains the same perspective with which she perceives the senior student, she is almost guaranteed to have a failed marriage. If she views her husband from this perspective, she's likely to come to a point where she detests her husband. Imagine that she cooks for her husband, but he doesn't help her prepare meals, doesn't finish all the food on the table, doesn't help with the dishes, and says he is busy when she asks him to do the dishes. She assumes he really is busy, but when she checks on him, she finds him idling on the computer or watching TV. If her husband continues to behave this way, she will end up despising him and will not be able to stay in the marriage.

If she continues with the same mindset that she has toward the senior student, she is likely to view all the people around her in a negative light. For instance, when she gets a job, she's likely to end up despising her boss and coworkers, so she won't be able to remain in any job for long.

She is also likely to have problems dating. If she writes to her boyfriend twice, but he only responds once, or if she calls him three times, but he only calls her once, she'll get into an argument with him.

All humans have selfish tendencies. People generally make phone calls when they need something. I myself rarely ever call someone to ask, "Do you need anything?" I usually call someone when I need help, and most of the calls I receive are from people who have some kind of request.

It's easy to think "Gosh, this person only calls me when they need something." However, most people behave this way. Do politicians fawn over their constituents all the time? No. They do that only during election campaigns to get votes. How come we don't detest all those politicians?

It's up to the senior student to choose to share her snack with the person right next to her and not with the younger student. It's her right to decide. It has nothing to do with you. It would be better to think, "I'm thankful when she gives me some, but if she doesn't, that's fine too." You need to think this way.

It's only natural for the senior to ask the younger student questions about things she doesn't know. People ask me questions when they are curious about something, and I also ask questions of others when I need to know something. People in this world give and receive help.

When you're always calculating the gains and losses in your interaction with others, life becomes very tiresome. Parents give their children 100%, but the children don't give their parents even 10%. Parents would be miserable if they expected their children to give them 100%. The fact is that these parents probably also received 100% from their own parents.

If we can calculate the total amount of help that we give

and help that we receive throughout our lives, the two will be about the same. If we consider the whole, there are people like the senior student who take more than they give, and there are other people who will benefit you much more than you benefit them.

If someone offers you a snack, take it and say, "Thank you." If they don't offer you any, just think, "That's okay." They are doing whatever they want to do with what is theirs, so why should you get annoyed?

The same goes for dating. You might like someone, but you shouldn't despise them for not returning your feelings. You have the freedom to like someone, and the other person has the freedom to like whomever they wish.

There's not even a need for you to resent your partner when they develop feelings for someone else. Feelings change, and there isn't much you can do about it. If that happens, rather than being resentful, instead, try to think, "Well, I have been happy for the past two years thanks to you. Thank you." Then, even though the situation is difficult, you don't have to suffer from feelings of betrayal.

The human psyche consists of both altruism and selfishness. During a crisis, people sometimes exhibit altruism, but they cannot be altruistic all the time. This is because altruism resides deeper in the subconscious than does selfishness. Thus, selfishness emerges more easily and more often.

Once you acknowledge the fact that all humans have a selfish side, you can then focus on deciding to what extent you will accommodate the demands of a selfish person. It's all up to you.

We don't need to rid ourselves of selfishness to achieve peace in the world. Simply understanding that others can be selfish just as we are will drastically reduce conflicts.

Don't condemn or try to change others. How do you expect to change others when we can't even change ourselves? However, it's all right to encourage others to change themselves for their own good, and not because we currently disapprove of them.

Before you begin, you should know that it's very hard for any person to change. In general, you feel annoyed if someone doesn't correct their behavior after you point it out once or twice. It may make you feel like they are ignoring your advice. If you feel this way, you need some introspection. Ask yourself, "Am I really trying to change them for their own sake? Is it possible that I want to change them because I dislike their behavior?"

Be prepared to wait for change. If you give advice to someone without expecting a quick change in their behavior, you won't feel annoyed, even if that person doesn't change. Because you know that it's extremely hard for people to change in any way, you can continue to remind them and support the process of change.

You shouldn't become stressed just because they don't listen to you. If the advice was for their well-being and not for your own, and they choose not to listen, it's their own business. There's no need for you to get upset. If you become stressed, it means that, although you say, "I'm changing them because it will be good for them," in reality, you gave them the advice to fulfill your own needs.

"Your opinion is wrong, so change it." You should not force your thoughts on others. You can tell them what you know, but you must leave it to them to decide for themselves. You can usually point out that others are wrong and try to change them, but this leads to conflict. Also, when they don't change, you'll become annoyed. "They still haven't come to their senses." If you think this way and become angry, you are the one who suffers.

If you get angry and annoyed that others are not taking your advice, calmly observe your own mind. Upon introspection, if you think that you truly want to help them change for their own sake, just give them the necessary information and leave them to decide for themselves. Refrain from trying to reform them in your own way. Then, unnecessary conflicts will decrease drastically.

Give-and-Take Is
a Transaction, Not Love

The expression "give-and-take" signifies a mutual exchange. The act of giving and taking seems to be fair and natural in personal relationships, but in reality, it's closer to a business transaction. If you consciously do things for other people, you start to expect something in return, and you'll likely become unhappy if those expectations are not met. Even when you believe that you're doing something to benefit others, chances are you aren't doing what they truly want, and you may mistakenly overestimate the value of your actions to those people, which inevitably leads to conflict.

Imagine a husband buys an outfit for his wife, and she

doesn't seem to appreciate it. He will immediately feel disappointed. He may ask, "Honey, why don't you wear the outfit that I got for you?" She may answer, "I don't think it looks good on me." Then, he may ask angrily, "What? I went to a great deal of trouble to get it for you. Is that all you can say?" Disappointment and resentment can arise instantly. We can observe how frequently this happens—not just between lovers but also with family and friends.

A woman once consulted me about feeling sad and disappointed in her family: "I live abroad, far away from my family, so I often call my siblings in Korea. But they never call me, even on special holidays. I want to know how they're doing, but I think to myself, 'Why should I be the one to call every time?' So, I haven't called them recently. I feel frustrated." This is like saying, "What goes around should come around. If I called ten times, they should call me back at least once."

Many people will empathize with this statement. But we are forgetting something important. We call our families because we're concerned about them and want to know how they are doing. That is, we call because we want to call them rather than for their sake. It's not a sin not to call your siblings or your parents. If you want to call them, call them, but if you don't want to call, you don't have to.

Deciding not to call your siblings or parents because they don't return the favor is no different from trying to engage your family in a business transaction. It seems like an unfair deal to you, so you're standing your ground and not calling them.

Saying, "I've done this for you, but what have you done for me?" is no different from a business transaction. It's not a problem if you do something for others because you want to, but if you wish to receive something in return, your relationship is likely to go sour. If your expectation goes unfulfilled, you'll become increasingly disappointed and get into conflict with others. It would be wiser to call your family and frankly express your feelings: "I feel hurt that I'm the only one calling everyone in the family."

The reason that conflicts arise among people who are close is because of the desire to receive as much love as one gives. When you love someone, there is a good chance you'll be loved back. But if the love is not reciprocated, you may feel very unhappy and betrayed. You may lament, "Why did I give so much love to someone who wouldn't love me back?"

Here, we must take note that the reason our love leads to hatred and disappointment is not because of the other person, but because of our desire to receive as much as we give. Thinking, "I'm doing this for you" will inevitably lead to a feeling of resentment and the question, "I go out of my way for you, but what have you done for me?"

If you realize that doing things for others is actually for your own happiness, you will not expect anything in return and will naturally not feel any resentment. It's best to stop engaging in business transactions with your loved ones; instead, you should cultivate a genuine relationship with them.

Life Will Feel Empty
If You Live with a Sense of Responsibility

They say a parent's love for their child is unconditional and pure. But when times are tough, even parents say things like, "I've gone through so much to raise you." This translates to an underlying expectation: "I've worked hard to raise you, so you owe it to me to take care of me when I'm old." As a result of this belief, some parents end up resenting their children.

If parents fully enjoy the experience of raising their children, they wouldn't feel sad even if their children didn't fulfill any filial obligations once they grew up. Since parenthood already brought them so much joy, it wouldn't even cross their minds that they did anything for their children, or that their children owe them anything. They would simply be happy and grateful when their children get settled and begin their own lives. When parents subconsciously think, "I raised you," they become disappointed in their children and bring suffering upon themselves.

I met a man who lived alone while supporting his wife and child, who were living overseas. He came to ask me for advice, saying that even though it was a good decision to send his family overseas for the sake of his child's education, sometimes his life felt purposeless. "I feel pleased about my child studying overseas, but occasionally, I feel so empty. How can I free myself from this feeling and become a better father and breadwinner for my family?"

If the purpose of your life is to fulfill obligations, you may think that you're doing your best, but you are also likely to feel that your entire life is pointless and empty. Asking yourself the question. "What kind of a father should I be for my child?" may sound noble, but the hidden meaning behind it's that you are sacrificing yourself for your family. Over time, you will become stressed and unhappy.

"I'll devote myself to my family."

"I'll make sacrifices for my children."

People who say these things have a sense of duty in their hearts. This sense of duty weighs heavily. If you feel burdened, you have to honestly ask yourself whether you like living alone or whether you prefer living together with your family.

If you feel that it's indeed better to be married than to be alone, and that it's better to have children no matter how much trouble they may be, you're mistaken in thinking you are sacrificing yourself for your wife and child. Rather, you should say to your child, "Thank you. I'm happy because you're in my life." To your wife, you should be able to say, "Although you may nag me sometimes, life is fun thanks to you." If you feel grateful to your wife and children, you'll have a happy family life, and you will naturally become a good father and husband.

Many parents sacrifice their lives to support their adult children, but there is a limit to making sacrifices. Eventually, they may start to wonder if it's necessary to live this way and ask themselves why they should live a life of hardship, tied down to a family. Furthermore, if you think you are sacrificing for someone, you'll eventually want to be compensated. You may think, "Is that the best you can do when I'm working so hard for you?" As your disappointment grows, you end up lamenting your fate. Thus, devoting your life to others is a far cry from living a free and happy life.

Being a good parent is no different from being a good spouse. No matter how devoted parents are and how much money they spend on their children, if parents argue and scream at each other, their children are more likely to go down a troubled path. If both parents are happy in their marriage, their children are more likely to turn out well. Even children who don't achieve noteworthy success in school may later grow up to be successful.

Ultimately, living together as a happy couple is the way to be good parents, so it's better for parents to live together. Parents living happily together and sending their child to any school is better than living separately and sending their child to a prestigious school.

When parents make sacrifices for their children, expectations about their children grow, so the children end up with heavy emotional burdens. As a result, the children may lose enthusiasm for life and become overly conscious about what their parents may want. Even when children become older and begin their own families, it's very likely that they will continue to depend on their parents instead of becoming independent. If you truly wish for your children's happiness and want to be good parents, you must encourage them to be fully independent when they turn twenty years old.

"I'll feed you, put a roof over your head, and pay for your education until you graduate from high school. After that, you can live your life as you please." You could add, "It doesn't matter to me whether you decide to live alone or get married, and I'll accept whomever you want to marry. Live as your heart desires. I support your decisions."

Children will be able to live energetically when you set them free to venture into the world. These days, however, many children are raised within restrained environments and conditions, and most of them lack spirit. The youth of our time are generally conservative, seeking only to be secure and avoiding challenges, which can stagnate the whole society.

Children grow up well anywhere. Parents don't need to worry about them. However, if parents feel that raising a child is painful, it will be difficult for the child to become successful. How can a child who brings pain to their parents ever become successful?

If you consider that parenting is a sacrifice, it may feel like a shackle. Let go of the thought that "I'm doing all of this for you." Then, both you and your child can lead a happy life.

Dependence is
the Seed of Resentment

People seem to have unrealistically high expectations and many fantasies about marriage, perhaps because of the increasing consumption of movies, dramas, and fictional stories about love. People think if they get married, they will be blissfully happy. Such high expectations lead to equally large disappointments, so many couples clamor to get out of their marriage not long after tying the knot.

Instead of thinking of marriage simply as two people living together, people expect to have a romantic and passionate marital relationship like in movies or books. They become unhappy when their spouses don't shower them with undivided attention and love. They may have experienced heart-fluttering moments when they were dating, but after marriage, they find being with each other dull, and they don't have much to talk about. Even though their spouses are neither bad nor significantly lacking, they may complain, saying, "We don't talk as much as we used to when we were dating, and things are dull. This is not how a marriage should be..."

Cooked rice has no special flavor, but it's good for your health. Alternatively, fast food might taste good, but it's detrimental to your health. Likewise, someone who is married might feel happy saying, "My husband loves me passionately; he can't live without me." But this happiness is confined within a fence that the husband has built. If the wife were to take one step outside the fence, her husband would be devastated. This is the happiness of a bird locked in a cage.

A woman once asked me for advice because she felt distressed by her obsession over her husband: "I don't know how to let go of my desire to rely and depend on my husband. I'm afraid that if I let go of it, I'll start obsessing over my children instead."

Obsessive attachment comes from dependence. From a positive perspective, depending on someone means trusting that person. From a negative perspective, it's being servile, because our joys and sorrows depend on the other person's actions. You mistake it for love and attention, but it's actually an obsessive attachment, and the object of your obsession can keep changing.

If you can't let go of your obsession over your husband, and you shun him because you're hurt, the object of your obsession will shift instead to your children. This is very burdensome for your children and will be a source of future conflict with them.

One positive aspect of a marriage is that spouses are able to rely on each other to ease their loneliness. But when they're overly dependent on each other, their marriage becomes a burden and can even feel like a shackle. Rather than the marriage itself, it's the state of being overly dependent on each other that confines the husband and wife.

In general, those who feel that they were not sufficiently loved by their parents might fall easily for anyone who is even a little bit nice to them. They try to compensate for the love they feel they didn't receive from their parents by seeking it from a love interest or a spouse.

Initially, it can seem like the love they didn't receive as children is being fulfilled by the marriage. But with time, they will gradually grow disappointed and resentful toward their spouses. They then turn to their children in an attempt to fulfill their desire for the love that was not satisfied by their parents or spouses.

Unfortunately, they'll likely be disappointed by their children as well, since they don't turn out the way they expected them to. As a result, they end up resenting their parents, despising their spouses, and feeling betrayed by their children. At this point, they may feel like they're living in hell. They started off by resenting their parents, and while wandering through life in search of a person to rely on, they also ended up despising their spouses and children.

Being dependent on someone means that your life changes course based on their attitudes and actions, and this is bound to create suffering. It's like tying yourself up with several ropes, giving one to your parents, one to your spouse, and one to each of your friends, so you're dragged in all directions depending on which way they pull you.

If you depend on others like this, you end up losing your

own perspective, judgment, and sense of autonomy. Tethered to those around you, you're bound to be in a constant state of confusion and distress.

Generally, our idea of love includes the tendency to depend on the person we love. But true love means loving others while being independent. Be ready to provide help and refuge to those whom you love without expecting anything in return. When we make sacrifices for the sake of those we love while expecting something in return, we will inevitably end up feeling resentful.

We rarely become enemies with strangers. Rather, it's our loved ones who become our sworn enemies because our dependence on and expectations of them turn our love into hate. Starting today, break your habit of depending on others and imprisoning yourself and others in the name of love. Live with the mindset, "I am the master of my own life."

Stop Interfering
in Other People's Lives

Sometimes our concern for other people—especially those close to us—becomes excessive, to the point that we interfere in their lives. Our status as someone's parent, child, or relative often becomes the justification for such interference. We meddle in their affairs, thinking that we are helping, but they might feel burdened by our behavior. Our eagerness to assist can bring suffering to both ourselves and to others.

A woman who was worried about her unmarried, unemployed children once asked me for advice: "My son and daughter are both in their thirties. Although they have searched for four years, they've failed to get jobs. They've been trying very hard, so I can't understand how they haven't succeeded. On top of that, neither is married. I'm very concerned about them. What should I do?"

It's common for parents to worry about their children. They think, "She should find a good job," or "He should get married soon." These parents are just expressing their concern for their children, but the children often find it burdensome. After your children turns 20, you should let them manage their own affairs, whether the topic is about work or relationships. I'm not telling you to stop loving your children; you should just stop interfering in their lives.

When I give this type of advice, some people reply, "But isn't that being uncaring and apathetic?" Others ask whether this contradicts the Buddha's teachings, which instruct us to love and look after all living beings. When I tell people to refrain from interfering in others' lives, I'm not advising them to be indifferent toward their families or the world. What I mean is that they should respect their children and start seeing them as independent and autonomous individuals.

Of course, all children need to be cared for. Throughout their preschool, elementary school, and middle school years, children must be nurtured and carefully guided. Parents are responsible for taking care of their own children. If there is a child without biological parents, another adult should step in and take on the role of caregiver. Regardless of blood relationships, every child needs to be looked after by an adult.

As children grow older and reach adolescence, they change physically. At the same time, they develop a stronger sense of individuality and seek to do things on their own. Where once they might have once followed their parents' words without question, eventually they become more assertive. Teenagers become interested in doing things that parents forbid, while resisting doing what their parents ask of them. So, conflicts arise between parents and their teenage children. However, this is quite natural.

During adolescence, children begin to make their own decisions and go through different experiences. In the process, they make mistakes, have heartaches, and get hurt, which helps them mature. Although parents may be worried, they should stand back and give their children space. This is true love. If parents continue interfering in their children's lives, in addition to causing conflicts, they will rob their children of many opportunities to grow through their own experiences. As children grow into adulthood, parents must completely relinquish their attachment. This is the only way that children can mature to become fully independent individuals.

Parents shouldn't be overly involved, nor completely indifferent toward their children. They should love their children but only provide support when their kids ask for help.

Offering pertinent advice to someone who comes to me for help out of frustration yields positive results. However, offering unsolicited advice is never taken well by anyone and will have negative results. If I offered too much unsolicited advice, people would be loath to come see me at all, let alone ask me for help. Instead, they would think, "I wonder what Sunim will scold me about this time?" Thus, unsolicited advice has many adverse effects.

If you take the attitude that, "Do whatever you want. I don't care," when others don't listen to you, you're being negligent and apathetic. Both providing unsolicited help and not providing help when asked will undermine the trust people have in you. Neither interference nor indifference is helpful to others. Sometimes we think, "Should I leave her alone?" or "Should I correct him?" These kinds of thoughts come from our desire to interfere. You may want to help, but if the other person wants to try to do something on their own, it's best to wait and see how that goes.

The same principles apply to romantic relationships. When you have strong feelings for someone, you may want to offer them unsolicited help. This behavior is born of ignorance. If you want your interest to be reciprocated, you must refrain from acting on impulse, and instead be able to observe patiently. Waiting until your loved one actually needs help or requests it is true love.

It's generally good to help those in need, but there are things you need to keep in mind. For one thing, it's better to provide help to others when they actually need it. If you help others because you feel they need help, you may bring trouble upon yourself. Also, blaming yourself for not being able to help those in need will only make you unhappy. It's good to help when you can, but if you can't, that's okay too.

It's actually dangerous to assume that you can help or teach others because it's easy to fall into the trap of trying to help others out of self-interest, or to show off. If you are trying to comfort a person who is dealing with a difficult situation, and you observe your own mind carefully, you'll find that you are actually motivated by self-interest. If you really want to help others, you must first listen to them attentively, and then share any relevant experiences you may have had.

Trying to impose your views on other people's lives only creates unnecessary trouble for yourself. Whether it's your parents, siblings, or children, once you start meddling in their lives, your own life will become exhausting. If you feel drained from helping others, it means that your desire to interfere in other peoples' lives has outstripped your ability to actually help them. This is a sign that you need to take a step back and let everyone live their own lives. Instead of giving unsolicited assistance, wait until it's requested, and then help in the best way you can. That way, you will be helpful to others and enjoy a more leisurely life.

All the Trees Together
Make a Forest

When you go to the mountains, do you find only one kind of tree or many kinds of trees? You'll see broadleaf trees as well as pine trees. You can even find smaller trees growing underneath tall trees. Amidst the diversity and differences, they grow together harmoniously.

If this is so, then why do conflicts arise between people who get married because they love each other? Do they occur because of the husband's bad habits? Do they happen because of the wife's nagging? These are not the true sources of conflict. When the husband does what he likes, and his wife asks, "Why do you do this all the time? It's bad for your health and wastes money. How can you do something so stupid?" The husband may respond with, "There you go again. Stop nagging!" Conflicts arise when partners antagonize each other in this way.

It all comes down to the thought, "I'm right. You're wrong," which inevitably leads to conflict. Humankind is as diverse as trees in the forest. Our thoughts and preferences are as diverse as people's physical appearances.

To live in harmony, we need to acknowledge our differences. You want to go out, and your partner might want to stay in. You might like someone, but that person might not like you. Everyone sees things from their own point of view. When we insist on our own perspectives, we can't avoid friction. We fight because we mistakenly think others are wrong, when they are merely different.

If people think of themselves as the center of the universe and try to measure others against their own subjective standards, even married couples are bound to fight. If we recognize and understand each other's differences, we should be able to avoid conflict, even if we were to move in with someone we just met on the street.

What if an employer and employee understood each other's

perspectives right from the beginning? The employee might realize, "I guess my boss would like to save on labor costs." The employer might think, "I guess my employee would like to be paid a little bit more." Each could understand the other in this way. This is not necessarily the same as agreeing with one another. If each understood the other, there would be room for negotiation.

If somebody insults you, it's difficult to listen with a sense of humor. But imagine if someone started talking in his sleep and said, "I can't stand Pomnyun Sunim." What would I do? Would I get angry, wake him up, grab him by the collar and yell, "What did you just say to me?" I wouldn't do that. I would just laugh and say, "Wow, he talks a lot in his sleep."

Interpersonal friction caused by differences in opinion isn't very different from talking in your sleep. In both cases, people are caught up in their own thoughts, and they're not able to rid themselves of ignorance. When we understand this, we can smile and let it go. Understanding other people must take priority over any effort to get them to change their behavior. If people need to improve themselves, it's better to provide them with the opportunity to realize it on their own.

For example, your spouse might refuse to do any work

around the house. If you understood him, you might think, "That's all right" or "At least he works hard at his job." If you believe that he needs to help with housework in order to set a good example for the children, there are some things you could try. You could ask for help by saying, "Honey, I feel too tired to get out of bed. Could you get me a cup of coffee?" If you were to abruptly demand, "Why do I always make the coffee? You make it this time!" you'd likely start an argument. Rather, you could create an opportunity for him to help out by saying in a weak voice, "Honey, I'm hungry. Could you cook something for me?"

It's extremely difficult to change someone. Adjusting to the other person is the quickest and least painful solution to most issues. If you seek to change someone despite knowing that people don't change easily, you'll need to have a lot of affection and wisdom. Instead of forcefully trying to change someone who doesn't want to change, you need to learn to induce change wisely.

If you feel unhappy in your relationship with others, try changing your point of view. Try to look for their good points rather than their shortcomings. When you make an effort to view others in a positive way, you'll notice more things about them for which to be thankful, and you will be one step closer to happiness.

PART 04

DO NOT BUILD YOUR HAPPINESS ON OTHER PEOPLE'S MISFORTUNE

Our current society is extremely competitive. People commonly believe, "I can only survive if I defeat you." As they seek to obtain better positions and more profits, there is bound to be more conflict and strife. People think they'll be happy when they win and unhappy when they lose. Therefore, everyone tries to become a winner by defeating others.

However, this so-called happiness is fundamentally built on the misfortune of others. While we rejoice at passing an exam, others are crying bitterly because they failed it. While we're delighted about winning an election, others are in despair due to their loss. While we celebrate making a successful bid, others will be troubled by it.

There are people who have stable, high-paying jobs at big corporations. But at the same time, there are those who have unstable low-paying jobs. Also, there are many who haven't been able to find a job and who suffer from unemployment.

However, we blindly run on in our lives thinking, "I'm okay, as long as this doesn't happen to me." But what is waiting for us at the end of the track where we're sprinting like racehorses?

What Is
True Success?

Everyone dreams of a successful life. Then, what is true success? A twenty-seven-year-old man asked me a question: "My criteria for success have been changing every year. Two years ago, it was earning an annual salary of over $30,000. A year ago, I became a tax accountant. I'm preparing for the public appraiser certification test. My current criteria for success is passing this test. My question is, what is true success in life?"

I asked him a question in return. "Is passing the test a success and not passing the test a failure? What are you going to do if you fail?"

"I want to continue to study for the test."

"Why do you want to be successful?"

"I want to make money."

"Why do you want to make money?"

"To live more affluently, I think."

"What is an affluent life?"

"Living in a big house."

"It will be difficult to maintain a big house."

"But I want to have the life of the affluent."

"Why do you want to live in a big house? Do you like showing off?"

"Yes, to some extent."

"What is good about showing off a big house?"

"I guess there's nothing good about showing it off."

As you can see from this dialogue, many people work hard to succeed, but when they're asked why they want to succeed, their answers are often vague. If I continue to press them for an answer, they say, "To be happy." That's right. Ultimately, we want to be happy and free. But what if we waste so much time chasing happiness that we die without ever experiencing it?

This young man said that his criteria for success were to

pass the test for which he'd been preparing. If he is studying to achieve a goal, he should be happy about the process of studying itself. However, we suffer while studying and think that we succeed only if we pass the test. The process of hiking up the mountain should make us happy, but we suffer in the process of climbing up and feel happy only when we reach the top of the mountain. Is it a failure if we can't reach the top? No. If we reach only half-way up the mountain, we have achieved that much.

Still, we run ahead with all our strength without thinking about where we're going. What kind of success are we working so hard to achieve?

One day, a doctor said he was worried because he didn't have many patients. So, I asked, "Should people get sick so that you can make money?"

How can he be a genuine doctor when he wants people to be sick? These days, many people seem to want to become doctors, not because they want to make people well, but because they want to make money. Some doctors are suspected of over-diagnosing and over-treating patients in order to increase their profit, so there are many people who don't trust doctors.

The situation is similar with lawyers. Since it's hard for lawyers to make money working for marginalized people who aren't protected by the law, they flock to large law firms that make money by helping these companies evade taxes. This is because their goal is to make money. Why do people waste their precious talent to become slaves to money? Is that true success?

The world is crazy about money, and the only religion people truly believe in seems to be the "money religion." As the world revolves around money, people are likely to betray the trust of others if they can make money. For instance, some people may leave their partners for wealthier people. People don't hesitate to leave the company they worked at for over 30 years to move to another company that offers them a higher salary. They may seem shrewd, but they're actually all slaves to money.

So, how should success be defined for people to be happy? A doctor's calling is to treat patients. A good doctor is someone who prevents people from becoming sick. A doctor's ultimate goal should be to have no patients. It's the same for lawyers. A good lawyer should be someone who helps clients who are seeking divorce not to divorce. When you work for people's happiness rather than for money, your life can be deemed successful.

Most people think that making a lot of money and living in a big apartment in a large city is a successful life. But, even if you live on a farm in the countryside, if you can be satisfied with your life and think, "I'm so happy to be free to do the work I want while enjoying the fresh air," your life is successful.

However, since people have misconceptions about success, they live their lives trying to meet other people's standards. Others might view them as successful, but they're likely to become mentally exhausted. That's why, when people are old or sick, they feel their life's accomplishments were futile rather than worthwhile. I'm not saying that people shouldn't study or work hard. What I mean is that people shouldn't waste their lives on pursuing false success, because later, when they look back on their lives, they may regret it.

True success starts with knowing that each moment is valuable and precious. No matter what situation you're in, you should be able to enjoy your life under the given circumstances. So, you need to constantly check whether you're happy in the here and now.

If we can maintain such a perspective, we can lead a life that was successful yesterday, is successful today, and will be successful tomorrow.

Do Not Build Your Happiness
on Other People's Misfortune

For many people, their goal in life is to become successful. Generally, being successful involves graduating from a good college, getting a good job, and marrying well. Graduating from a prestigious university is supposedly the key to finding a good job. A good job is supposedly one that has a light workload, pays well, has good benefits, holds authority, and invites the envy of others. In short, being successful is having more wealth, status, prestige, and popularity compared to those around you. Of course, when we talk about success in such a frank manner, some might shake their heads and say, "That's not always the case."

Usually, people don't think that their success has harmed others. Unfortunately, this is far from the truth. If you live in an apartment that is 2,000 square feet, and people around you call you rich, this means that they probably live in a smaller apartment, and they feel deprived by comparison. This can be considered happiness built on the misfortune of others, but the thought doesn't even occur to us.

Most people think that simply having more of anything than others, whether it be money, power, prestige, or fame, is the key to a successful life. They think that having more will also enable them to be generous to others later. That is, they think they'll be able to donate more, give more to their church or temple, operate a big charity organization, and do important things that will enable them to mark their name in history.

The problem is that "having more" is a relative concept. For you to have "more" than others, there needs to be someone else who has "less" than you. Let's use wealth as an example. For someone to work less and get paid more, another person has to work more and get paid less.

The same goes for power. If there is someone giving an order, another person needs to take the order and carry it out. Thus, for one person to succeed, a great many have to fail, and the greater the wealth of one person, the greater the number of people who can't even satisfy their basic needs.

In the end, the success we pursue is fundamentally achieved by passing on suffering to others. Today's society is particularly structured in a way that you can only achieve success through the sacrifice of others. Your success is inevitably followed by another person's failure, so it's not realistically possible for everyone to succeed together. This is because our society currently consists of a pyramid structure where one person's gain leads to another one's loss. People hustle to seize the top spot in the pyramid, and when a few secure the top spots, the majority of the people are relegated to the position of supporting them.

Even if the top-level positions are filled with very smart people, the pyramid will crumble if there aren't any people in the middle and bottom positions providing support. The few people on top are able to reach the top because most people function merely as stepping stones.

However, those at the top take their privilege for granted, thinking that they got there because they deserved it. They may even dismiss those supporting them from below as incompetent. Thus, most people think that any position other than the top is meaningless and they seek to reach the highest level at any cost.

In a society like this, it's easy for those who satisfy their own desires at all costs to be recognized as examples of success. These days, those who work hard and care about others are ignored as being naive, while those who live idly from receiving a large inheritance are envied and considered lucky.

When there are people around you who are suffering, but you have more money, power, honor, and popularity than others, the pleasure you derive from all you own is gained at the cost of their sacrifice. Therefore, you must realize that you're able to work less and live in comfort because there are people who work harder and still live in poverty.

One day, King Prasenasit asked the Buddha, "How do I become a great king?" And the Buddha answered, "Love your subjects as you would love your only son. You mustn't build your happiness on other people's misfortune. Do not regard the position of a king as something special. If you always help the poor and the sick and comfort the lonely, you don't need to leave home and lead the ascetic life of a monk. If a king is foolish, it's difficult to preserve his own life, much less a whole country."

In general, we think that a great leader should be powerful. But the Buddha emphasized that King Prasenasit should not consider being a king something special and that caring for the people is the most important qualification and virtue of a leader.

As the prince of a kingdom, the Buddha had led a life of luxury. But after witnessing the suffering of the common people, he gave up his enviable life like it was an old shoe and left home. When he made this decision, he decided not to follow a path of taking away others' possessions to fill his own storehouse, or of taking away another's position to promote his own success. He did not take away another's honor to gain his own.

But we've mistakenly believed that succeeding in life constitutes building our happiness on others' misfortune. We've pursued it blindly, thinking that this would make us happy.

Moving forward, what do we need to do so that everyone can become happy together? Even though we live in a competitive society, the way to win without oppressing others and to lose without feeling defeated is to set your life goals to come second rather than first. For example, if there is an opportunity for a promotion, look to your colleague and wish for them to get promoted instead. When they hear this, some might ask, "Won't I lag behind in life if I do that?"

Actually, that's not the case. What I'm trying to say is that you should refrain from obsessing over getting the promotion. I'm not saying that you shouldn't work hard on your job. You should work very hard, but when there is an opportunity for promotion or reward, give way to others.

For example, let's say you went somewhere to sell products and a competitor showed up. Telling the customer to consider buying his competitor's products first is not entirely for the sake of the competitor. Rather, it's for your own sake.

If you could genuinely feel that way, you wouldn't be stressed by the competition, regardless of whatever choice the customer makes. You wouldn't feel defeated even if the customer buys your competitor's product. Should the customer choose to purchase your product even after you recommend your competitor's product, that's the choice of the customer; you don't have to trample on your competitor.

However, if you can't adopt this altruistic attitude and

feel that you have to compete against others, you just need to face the consequences. Because if you trample on your competitor today, someday they'll reciprocate. No one can avoid the consequences of their actions. Therefore, you will suffer less if you can accept the consequences willingly. Then, you won't feel so resentful or victimized.

If we are awakened to how life works, we can become successful, have a comfortable life, and also make money. However, we lead weary lives because we try to defeat others at any cost, without understanding the true ways of the world.

If you don't have the desire to win, you don't need to be nervous or anxious no matter who you meet. You'll be at ease no matter what you do and where you live, and you'll be able to get along with everyone.

Desire Is
Like a Burning Log

The capitalism that dominates the world we live in today is excellent at fulfilling human desires. However, there is an immense problem with this system: it not only fulfills our desires but encourages them to perpetually grow.

Back in the days when South Korea experienced food shortages, people who could afford to eat beef soup with white rice were considered to be well-off. When food became abundant, having nice clothes became a sign of wealth. Then, people's standards of affluence kept changing, from owning a car, to owning a house, and so on. People's desires continued to grow.

Even though people now enjoy more material abundance than ever before, they also want to own more things than ever before. We have so much, yet we think we need more, comparing ourselves with others. People are neither happier nor more generous than they were when they barely had anything. In fact, they have become more cold-hearted while competing to have more.

Moreover, South Koreans are obsessed with economic growth. Since the country has recorded steady economic growth during the past 50 years, people panic if the growth rate plateaus or decreases even slightly. This is because their preoccupation with working hard to bring about economic growth and to improve their lives, which began when South Korea was poor, still persists.

The truth is that however bad the current economic situation in South Korea may seem, people are leading far more affluent lives than those of 20 years ago. However, people also complain more, are more dissatisfied, and are unhappier. This is because our expectations of economic standards have also increased. With such a relative definition of success, it's no wonder that the feeling of deprivation endures, no matter how much the economy grows.

We now need to come to our senses and learn to live frugally. If we continue indulging ourselves in material consumption as we do now, what do you think will happen to Earth?

Human desire can't ever be satisfied. Whenever a desire is fulfilled, it only grows bigger. For example, even if you have always walked to school, once you try driving there in a car, you won't want to walk there again. Because of the way the human mind works, once we have ridden on an express bus, we don't want to go back to taking a regular bus. Once we get used to more convenience and comfort in our lives, it's hard to go back to the old ways.

As we get caught up in our desires, they take charge of our lives. When a desire is fulfilled, we temporarily feel high with happiness. That's because we think the more we have, the freer and happier we will be.

A college student asked me for advice because she was worried that she might have a shopping addiction: "I think I spend far more money than my peers. I keep a part-time job to fulfill my desire to shop. As I spend most of the money I earn, I get anxious if my income decreases even just a little bit although I still earn just as much as my friends. I feel inferior if I can't spend as much money as I usually do. I'm worried that I feel this way when I'm still quite young."

First and foremost, the fact that you have become aware that you're addicted to shopping and that you have a problem means that you are unhappy living the way you are now. It's fine if shopping makes you feel happy and free. However, if you can't stop shopping even when you feel shackled by it, this means you're addicted. For now, you hold on to the addiction because the amount of suffering it brings is still bearable. But soon, the time will come when you have no other choice but to quit.

As for me, when I'm invited to a big house, I look around and think, "Oh my, it must be tough to clean." But if you can't let go of the habit of perceiving bigger as better, you'll continue to want newer and bigger things. Eventually, you will try to satisfy your desire even if you have to take out a loan to do it.

If you feel nervous, anxious, or chronically dissatisfied with life, you're more susceptible to developing an addiction. You can't control your desire to shop, and you want to spend increasingly more money. To do that, you need to make more money, so you may keep changing your job to find something that pays more. You're essentially a slave to money.

When your addiction grows, you begin to engage in risky business to make money. You tell yourself, "Just this once," even though it weighs on your mind. You'll be tempted to take part in illegal activities if it pays twice or three times your usual pay.

Initially, almost no one who gets involved in illegal or unethical activity plans to do it long-term. People think, "I'll just do it this once" because they have an urgent need for money at the time. Once they make a sizable amount of money, they think they'll be set for a while, but it doesn't work out that way. As their income increases, their desire to spend increases even faster. Such risks lurk in a shopping addiction. Therefore, instead of waiting until you reach a dead end, you must quit the moment you recognize that it's a problem.

As your addiction becomes more serious, it will alter the way you think. Then, you'll begin to deceive yourself. It's almost impossible to detect the changes that you go through. Therefore, you must quit now that you have recognized the problem.

For instance, when you hunt, a jackrabbit will take bait

more readily in the winter than in the summer because food is more scarce when it's cold. People are no different. When they're caught in a desire for something, there is a high chance that they will seek to fulfill it without realizing that they will be suffering a great loss, just like a hungry rat taking the poisonous bait. In other words, food is a weakness to hungry people, bribery has power over those who want wealth, and flattery works on those who have a strong desire for power.

When you're blinded by greed, you are unable to make the right choice. In order to make the right choice, you must give up on satisfying your desire to a certain degree, but instead you run forward, only looking at the carrot hanging in front of your eyes.

Stop and look around to check where you're going. Make sure you're not running blindly toward the edge of a cliff in your quest to satisfy your desires.

Three Levels of Needs:
Need, Desire, and Greed

People are happy when their needs are satisfied. We feel good if we're doing something we want to do. We're satisfied when everything turns out the way we want. We feel happy when our needs are fulfilled but feel miserable when they're not.

These feelings of happiness and unhappiness all stem from needs. There are endless kinds of needs, such as the need to eat, to wear nice clothes, to have material possessions, to win, and so forth. But realistically, it's not possible to satisfy one's every need and desire. Take a family for example. If every member of the household did whatever they wanted, the family would end up breaking up, and all the members of the family would suffer. Thus, pursuing your desire can ultimately cause great harm to others as well as yourself.

However, a need in and of itself is not all bad. Everyone has needs, and sometimes, they can be a great driving force. We just have to understand the boundaries of those needs.

There are three types of needs. The first are physiological needs. These basic human needs include seeking food when hungry, sleeping when tired, warmth when cold, and coolness when hot. Because one's survival is threatened if these basic needs are not met, an individual has the right to satisfy these needs, and society must also ensure that its members are able to fulfill these basic needs.

Next, there are relative needs, which are desires. The desire to eat something more delicious, to own more than others, to obtain a higher status, to wear better clothes, and to live in a more comfortable environment, are relative needs. These desires arise in people as a result of comparing themselves to others. Such desires do not have a defining boundary. Therefore, these desires should be restrained, since they can never be fully satisfied despite our attempts to do so. People must be able to control their desire to a certain degree, and society should have regulations that can keep individual desires under control.

Finally, there are excessive needs, which can be referred to as greed. Overeating might satisfy your appetite, but it's bad for your health. Drinking too much and overworking to make more money stems from greed, so greed is harmful to people. Individuals need to protect themselves by letting go of greed, and society must regulate the greed of individuals in order to protect society.

As such, since satisfying needs is not only important to individuals but also influences on society as a whole, society must provide an appropriate arbitration between ensuring and restraining or restricting the fulfillment of needs. From the individual's perspective, fulfilling survival needs is a basic right, and everyone should be able to exercise that right. However, individuals must restrain their relative needs or desires as they are impossible to satisfy, and they must let go of excessive needs or greed.

From a societal perspective, the fulfillment of physiological needs is a basic human right, so society must ensure that every person's survival needs are met. On the other hand, desires should be restrained appropriately, and greed must be deterred through proper regulation.

A man said that he wanted to live frugally, but he had trouble putting it into practice: "In the past, I pursued a life of wealth and success. After listening to your Dharma talks, I have begun to think that I would like to lead a frugal life. However, when I think realistically about making a living and getting married, which would require me to purchase a car and a house, I feel I should save a lot of money, so I start obsessing about money again."

If you always ate everything you wanted, would that be beneficial or harmful to your health? We consume food to keep our bodies healthy, but often, food that is pleasing to the palate isn't necessarily healthy. There are foods that taste good but can harm the body, and there are foods that are not so palatable but will benefit the body. If you want to be healthy, sometimes, you should refrain from eating something you crave, and other times, you should eat something that you don't feel like eating. Food consumption should be focused on maintaining your health rather than pleasing your palate.

The same goes for wearing clothes. The purpose of wearing clothes is to protect our bodies. We dress to stay warm in cold weather and to protect our skin when the sun is blazing. Yet, those who wear expensive designer clothes are overly concerned that their clothes may be damaged. In fact, they protect the clothes rather than being protected by the clothes. They end up becoming slaves to their clothes.

The same applies to the house that we live in. As the size of your house gets bigger and holds increasingly more furniture and valuables, you end up protecting your house rather than being protected by your house. The house becomes the master, and you become the servant. When we blindly follow the desire for possessions, we end up losing control of our lives before we realize it.

If you're not careful, one day you'll find yourself living a life of servitude to all kinds of material things like clothing, food, houses, and so on. You must maintain awareness so that you're not dragged around by your desires.

Wanting to make money through employment or business isn't bad or being greedy. However, it's important to live modestly no matter how much money you make. Living frugally will enable you to save money. If you eat modestly, refrain from buying expensive clothing, and use public transportation, your monthly spending will be half of what your friends spend. So, for example, if your friends spend $2,000 per month, you'll only spend $1,000.

I'm not saying that you should be a cheapskate. I'm just telling you to avoid unnecessary spending. If you live modestly, your savings will increase. Therefore, living modestly and saving money for the future aren't contradictory.

Live your life based on a clear value system of your own instead of following other people's standards. If you don't think it's necessary to purchase a car, you can walk or take the bus even if everyone else travels by car. You don't need to buy a car simply because everyone else is doing it. Furthermore, when planning to get married, you should first find out whether your prospective spouse shares your values of living modestly rather than focusing on characteristics like height or appearance.

If you want to get married to someone who has different values and is more extravagant compared to you, you have to please that person. Then, you would have to pretend you're wealthy and put up a false front in order to attract that person.

However, if you do this, you're inviting disaster. Therefore, if you want to live according to your principles, you should get married when you meet someone who shares your life values. If you fail to meet someone compatible, you can opt not to get married. That way, you can avoid choosing a job solely based on pay or spending your life trying too hard to make more money. Then, you can be the master of your own life and do what you want to do.

You can live your life as you please in accordance with your values. However, because we live in a world full of people, there are a few rules that we should adhere to.

First, people can live their lives as they see fit, but no one has the freedom to cause harm to another. One should not harm or kill others. Second, people have the right to pursue their own interests, but they don't have the right to infringe on other people's interests. One should not extort valuables or steal from others. Third, people have the right to love and to be happy, but they don't have the right to harass another. One should not sexually abuse or assault others. Fourth, people have the right to speak freely, but they don't have the right to hurt others with words. One should not swear or lie. Fifth, people have the right to drink alcohol but do not have the right to get drunk and distress others. Therefore, one should not get intoxicated.

Other than these five rules, everyone can live their life as they please. You might say that this sounds simple enough.

However, the problem is that parents, who now have fewer children, are too protective of their children and fail to teach them basic ethics early on. Today's issues of violence at school include stealing, deceiving, and sexually harassing others, which all fall under the five precepts.

However, some parents adopt a vague attitude about their children's bad behavior that causes harm or loss to others. They fear that any kind of punishment will dishearten their children. But then, they scold their children for getting bad grades at school. Thus, children may come to believe that poor academic performance is worse than causing harm or loss to others.

Therefore, at home and in society, we should establish standards for controlling desires and teach them to our children. This is something we all need to do to coexist in this world.

The Individual Is the Seed
and Society Is the Field

In my Dharma Q&A talks, I consistently emphasize the importance of an individual's attitude and mindset. During one of these talks, an attendee objected and asked: "You've said that, as each of us strives to change ourselves, the world gradually becomes transformed through the accumulation of our individual efforts. Although this is a necessary ideal, exclusive focus on individual self-reflection leaves a lot to be desired. Flaws in the social system can cause human suffering and sacrifice. As systemic injustices become more entrenched, the world is becoming increasingly worse, so it's not right to emphasize change on an individual level without questioning the existing bad systems. Why is it that those exploiting the system do not reflect on themselves?"

No matter what circumstances we find ourselves in, we must go on living. This doesn't mean that we should unconditionally accept unfairness in the world. As long as we're alive, we need to continue striving to make the world a better place to live. However, society cannot change quickly or easily. That's why we must be able to accept current circumstances while simultaneously working to improve them.

I emphasize the importance of an individual's attitude and mindset because we have a strong tendency to blame others' behavior and external circumstances, rather than taking responsibility and thinking about what we can do on a personal level. Most of us look for happiness outside of ourselves. For example, we think that we'll be happier if our child gets better grades, if our spouse cuts back on their drinking, if our parents stop nagging, or if the world itself changes. However, does my desire for others to change cause them to change? Does complaining about the world cause it to improve? No, it doesn't.

Does this mean that I have no other choice but to suffer?

No, it doesn't. By changing my frame of mind, I can find freedom and happiness, regardless of the circumstances. That's why I tell people to refrain from blaming others. When we take control of our own lives, we become freer and happier.

A handful of beans were sowed in a field of gravel, and two of them grew to become sprouts. In situations like this, it's common for people to say, "Look, those that are fit to survive live." When a handful of beans were sowed in a fertile field, and every one of them survived except two, people say, "Look, those that are not fit to survive die."

They are saying that whether a seed sprouts or not depends only on the seed itself. However, if only 2% of seeds sown in a field of gravel sprouted, but 98% sprouted in a fertile field, this means that the quality of the field can also affect the seed's rate of survival.

For farming to be successful, it's not enough for the seeds to be good. The field must also be fertile. In the context of our lives, the seed is the individual, and the field is our society. Individual practice can be compared to making a good seed. Enriching the field can be compared to creating a good society.

When individuals are happy and social conditions are improved, we can become truly happy. Therefore, cultivating a society based on justice and general welfare is not separate from ensuring individual happiness.

Every January, I lead a Buddhist pilgrimage to India with hundreds of people. We all take the same bus, stay at the same hotel, and eat at the same restaurant. Despite traveling under the same conditions, I always find some people smiling the whole time, while others look extremely unhappy. When we get on a very uncomfortable truck, there's always someone who thinks it's fun and says, "Where would I be able to ride a truck like this?" Another person complains and says, "How can anyone in the modern world ride on such a vehicle?"

On the contrary, people's moods can change depending on the environment they are in. The way you feel in a smoke-filled, noisy place is different from the way you feel out in nature, surrounded by fresh air and clean water. The level of happiness you feel can differ based on the surrounding environment.

When we can't change the environment, we can change our frame of mind, to become happier than the previous day. This is practice. For example, you may have nagged your spouse to quit drinking for 20 years to no avail. Then, maybe if you change your mind and think, "Well, drink as much as you like," you'll feel less annoyed. Your spouse may drink just as much, but you will be happier based on your new mindset.

The root cause of your spouse's drinking may lie in the fact that no matter how hard he works, he is unable to improve his economic status. The problem may stem from socio-structural factors. In this situation, though it's important to feel compassion toward him instead of resentment, it's also important to take a step further and bring about social changes that will reduce his stress levels and drinking.

In current society, an extreme disparity exists between the rich and the poor. The majority of people – those who don't belong to the small, privileged class – will have an increasingly hard time making their ends meet. In addition to the quality of life actually getting lower, people are suffering more often from relative poverty.

Therefore, the situation will improve when economic polarization decreases. On the one hand, changing our own frame of mind is something we can strive for on an individual level. On the other hand, transforming systemic injustices, such as the gap between the rich and poor, cannot be accomplished through individual effort alone. Everyone in society must work together to bring about this kind of change.

Happiness depends on both our attitude toward life – our ability to deal with issues as they arise – and our environment. In order for happiness to be sustainable, both the seed (the individual) and the field (the society) need to be healthy. In sum, the individual and the society are the two wheels that pull the cart of happiness.

When Two Hunters Catch Three Rabbits

Why do humans live together when they fight one another over limited resources? Humans live together rather than alone because it's more beneficial for them. For example, when a man goes hunting alone, he may only catch one rabbit a day, but when two men go hunting, they may catch three rabbits a day. This is why humans cooperate with one another.

However, cooperation doesn't always yield good results. It's beneficial to cooperate when hunting, but conflict may occur when trying to divide the catch. In fact, as the number of people among whom the catch must be divided increases, conflicts manifest in many forms.

When many people get together and cooperate, it's likely that each of them will profit more than if they worked alone. However, there are some who get the short end of the stick. A prime example is the slaves in a system of slavery. When the number of people who suffer losses increases, and the anger and dissatisfaction of these people accumulate, society begins to crumble.

When an individual hunts and gathers food, the economy is about production. The concept of distribution doesn't need to be considered. For a while, when discussing the economy, Korea was only focused on production. However, when two or more people work together, distribution becomes as important as production.

Then, how should the three rabbits be distributed between the two hunters? Basically, each hunter should take one rabbit, but the question is how to divide the remaining extra rabbit that was caught thanks to the two hunters' cooperation. The minimum number of rabbits each hunter can take is one while the maximum number is two but not three.

In this situation, wanting to take one rabbit cannot be

considered greed since it's a person's basic right. Wanting to take more than one but fewer than two is a desire. Wanting to take more than two rabbits, even three, is greed. If you're greedy, you deprive others of their share, and sooner or later, you will suffer losses as well.

Therefore, individuals should refrain from being greedy, and social systems should regulate individuals acting on their greed. Also, social systems should ensure that a person's basic need, receiving that one rabbit, is fulfilled.

If social systems fail to regulate the greed of their people or ensure their basic rights, everyone in society will eventually suffer. If one hunter takes three, the other hunter won't get any. Since the latter hunter took a loss, he won't cooperate with the former hunter next time. In other words, the former hunter may have benefited by taking three rabbits on the first day, but he can't continue to benefit in the days that follow because the other hunter will no longer work with him.

Therefore, individuals need to compete for an adequate division of the extra rabbit. Ideally, each hunter should get one and a half rabbits each, but realistic variables need to be considered. For example, during the day's hunt, if you worked hard, but the other hunter was lazy, you may feel dissatisfied and have complaints if you shared the catch equally with the other hunter.

So, the rabbits could be divided into 1.2 vs. 1.8 or 1.3 vs. 1.7 pieces. Ideally, each hunter should receive 1.5, but realistically, that's not always possible. However, we need to continue to work for an equal distribution of 1.5 each.

Many of today's societal problems stem from the failure to ensure the basic rights of the disadvantaged and a lack of regulation of the greed of the privileged. Consequently, in society, there are many people whose survival is threatened and many who suffer from relative deprivation.

Unfortunately, at a time when South Korea should have sought social consensus on distributive justice, neoliberalism swept the country. After the foreign currency crisis of 1998, Koreans came to believe that adopting neoliberalism was the only way they would be able to survive, so Korean society became highly competitive. The most prominent characteristic of neoliberalism is winner-take-all. A typical example is the idea that one smart person can provide for 100,000 people. Encouraging competition in this way may increase productivity up to a certain degree, but there are limitations. Moreover, as income inequality intensifies, people will lose interest in working. As a result, the entire society can lose its driving force.

If one person can catch one rabbit, and two people can catch three by cooperating with each other, it's fair for each of them to get at least one but no more than two. The two hunters should reach an agreement that ensures each other's basic rights and, at the same time, minimizes relative deprivation.

If all the people in a community seek to fulfill their desire to have more, the community is sure to collapse. Ideally, each person should get one and a half rabbits. However, since it may not always be realistic to do so, it's necessary to adjust the distribution ratio according to each individual situation and the level of social maturity.

Become an Example First Before Criticizing Others

Most of us want to get paid a lot without necessarily working a lot. We want to get promoted even though we don't deserve it or get accepted into good colleges without meeting the academic qualifications. We desire a good seat even if we arrive late. And we want everyone to overlook our mistakes.

What if we learn to see these same situations from a different perspective? How would we feel if other people got salary increases while their workloads decreased, got promoted while performing their jobs poorly, or got accepted into great colleges with mediocre grades or test scores? We would feel outraged. We'd blame them for our difficulties and for our children being denied college admission.

When we have a wish, we usually don't think about the fact that our wish coming true means a loss for someone else. Even if it crosses our mind, we shake it off, thinking, "That's just the way life is." We turn a blind eye to it, convincing ourselves that everything is okay. We tell ourselves, "As long as I don't get the short end of the stick…"

At work, people are sometimes pressured to do something illegal, either to keep their jobs or to get promoted. At other times, they have to climb the corporate ladder, using coworkers as rugs. Expressing how painful it's to be faced with such choices, someone once asked me the following question:

"The media occasionally reports on companies involved with bribery using slush funds. The company I work for is involved in these types of practices. Although I feel ashamed, I have no choice but to implement such practices. How can I handle this situation wisely?"

You don't have to leave the company you work for just because the company's value system is different from yours. As long as the company doesn't ask you to leave, you can keep the job and do the right thing while you are working there. If you try to decide whether or not to quit, you can't help but hesitate. However, if you leave it up to the company to decide, you don't need to concern yourself with the decision. You become involved in conflicts when you criticize others, for example, when you say, "What you're doing is wrong," or "You are bad." In our lives, we will find problems wherever we look. Rather than criticizing others, it's important for us to resolve not to act like them.

If you're determined not to engage in illegal or unethical behavior, no matter how much the company pays you, you can leave your job. However, if you're unable to do so and choose to live as others do, you must accept the consequences willingly.

You need to understand in advance the consequences that may follow. If you help your company crush a competitor through unethical means, someday you may also be crushed in a similar way. Even if you are loyal to the company through this process, once the illegal slush fund is exposed, they can still throw you under the bus. Understanding this possibility in advance, be prepared to accept the consequences of your actions willingly rather than feel wronged and resentful. In the long run, you will see that immediate rewards are a poor measure of success.

If you don't want to suffer the repercussions, refrain from such actions that lead to them. You'll still be able to make a living. I met a civil engineer who once claimed that his job required him to drink every day. He said that he had to wine and dine clients in order to procure contracts. However, he quit drinking after participating in the "Awakening Retreat."• He later told me that he found he could still get contracts without drinking with his clients.

When trying to improve something, we often say, "Realistically, there isn't much I can do." In most cases, this is a hasty generalization, not based on an actual attempt. Someone might say that it's impossible to do business with clients without drinking with them. However, it's possible. If you have no choice but to go somewhere to drink with your clients, you can be there without having any drinks or can just pretend to drink. Also, you can do business with them without going to these events at all. At first, you might find yourself at a disadvantage and get fewer contracts. However, in the long run, if you're good at your job, you'll find a way

• A 5-day retreat program that guides people to experience changing their perspectives and begin their journey toward true happiness and freedom.

to make it work.

If your company encourages drinking and you try to avoid such occasions, your coworkers might complain, "It's the company night out. Where do you think you're going?" or "You're spoiling the fun." However, you can make a ground rule right from the start. If you say, "I will not drink," and stick to it no matter what, people will eventually accept it. If you say, "My dear colleagues, please excuse my absence," and seek understanding from those around you, you can stay on friendly terms with them. Since you're going against the organization's culture in order to stick to your values, you need to be apologetic. If you ride it out for about a year, things will sort themselves out.

On the other hand, if you are continually slipping out of company social events for personal reasons, while aggressively engaging only when promotion opportunities are available, your coworkers are likely to resent you. To foster cordial relationships with them, the opposite approach is needed. You can tell your colleague, "You go first." You can ask your boss to promote others before yourself by saying, "I'll wait for the next opportunity. I'm still young." If you adopt this attitude, you can head off potential conflicts in the workplace.

You will, of course, encounter a great deal of resistance and criticism in the beginning. Some coworkers may tell you to quit or warn you that you'll be passed over for promotions. However, if you persist and continue to live according to your principles, the people around you will start to change. As time goes on, they will start to accept and understand you. The problem is that you may not be able to endure it and give up prematurely.

If we put leading a happy life above money and social success, we have nothing to fear. We need to put up with a certain amount of loss and criticism. However, this isn't easy, so we tend to give up prematurely because we lack clear and guiding life principles.

When we're not centered, criticism bothers us. We need to pay attention to what others say to us, but we don't have to be restricted by it. We concern ourselves with what others say because we don't want to receive criticism. Since we don't want to be criticized, we always try to be nice to others.

You're born into this world and spend your life competing fiercely for a small gain. Let's say, one day, you find out that you are terminally ill, or you suddenly get fired from the company you've been devoted to for years. Imagine how angry and resentful you would feel. You may ask yourself, "What have I lived for?" You may feel that you've lived in vain. Therefore, this is definitely not a good way to live.

If you truly believe that bribery is unethical, you should refuse to engage in it. If you find that work-related drinking gatherings aren't beneficial, avoid them tactfully. At the same time, be the first to volunteer for unpleasant tasks, such as cleaning, and stop hankering after promotions. That is, maintain your principles while conceding secondary issues and doing things that others are reluctant to do. Then, your coworkers are more likely to support you than resent you.

When you want to overcome the contradictory realities in life and take the path that allows everyone to be happy, resolve to take the first step. If you become an example first, instead of criticizing others, you'll find hope and meaning in life.

How to Be Happy and Benefit Others
at the Same Time

Happiness that is obtained at the expense of someone else's happiness cannot last long. What then, is true happiness? Is there a way for us to all be happy together?

These questions plagued the Buddha 2,600 years ago before he left home in search of truth. He realized the inadequacy of a life based on acquiring material objects. That is, he discovered the truth that, as long as our primary goal is to possess more and more, we cannot be happy together.

Everyone wants to be happy. However, in the long run, happiness based on selfish desires leads to unhappiness and misery. Therefore, from this moment forward, we need to live lives that benefit others as well as ourselves. If you do things that benefit you while creating disadvantages for others, they won't continue to tolerate it indefinitely. On the other hand, if something benefits others but requires you to sacrifice, you won't be happy in that situation. Happiness is only sustainable when both parties benefit. Therefore, we need to work together to build a society where people pursue mutual benefits.

We need wisdom and courage to live a life that's good for us, as well as for others. For example, keeping a positive mindset at work is ideal. However, if you witness injustice at your workplace, you also need to be able to say, "Hey boss, this isn't right." You need to be someone who is principled and who quietly leads by example by volunteering to perform difficult tasks.

An office worker asked me a question on how to deal with discrimination against temporary employees at the workplace: "There are 30 people on my team. Only five are permanent employees, and the rest are temporary contract workers. Temporary employees are subject to discrimination in terms of pay and benefits compared to those with permanent positions. Therefore, I don't feel comfortable working with the temporary workers, and I feel bad for them. Some of them may be forced to leave the company when it's time for contract renewal. My heart feels heavy because I'm the one who has to terminate their contracts."

If you're not going to quit your job, it's not right to turn away from the task you're assigned to do, even if you're not happy about it. It's understandable that you don't feel comfortable about working with people who are discriminated against when they do the same amount of work. However, that is the current social system, and you can't change it all at once.

In any case, if it's a task that has been assigned to you, the best you can do is to explain the company policy to the temporary workers and be as fair as possible in the contract termination process. When some of the laid-off workers inevitably resent you, instead of trying to run away, lend them a sympathetic ear.

Also, your energy would be put to better use in devising ways to lay off fewer people than dreading and worrying about something that won't happen for several months. It would be better for you to spend your time either improving work efficiency or proposing creative ideas to increase the number of contract renewals.

We live in an unjust world. However, we need to try to make the world as fair as possible. That's progress. At the same time, we also need to acknowledge the inequality that exists as part of our current reality. If we insist on equality without acknowledging the inequality in the world, this becomes nothing more than a distant dream. Then, we won't be able to adjust in the real world. Conversely, if we accept the current inequality and settle without making any effort to encourage equality in the future, we won't be able to make any progress.

Thus, our feet must be firmly planted in the current unjust reality, but our goal should lie in working toward a more equitable world. Then, we'll find ourselves moving away from an unequal reality toward an equitable world one step at a time. When we take on this perspective, we can have a vision but also be realistic at the same time. That way, we'll be able to make our dreams come true in real life.

Realizing your dreams within the reality means first accepting your current conditions and then investigating ways to ensure that temporary workers are no longer discriminated against in your company.

For example, in the past, there used to be a significant wage gap between men and women. However, rather than taking it lying down, people made persistent efforts to narrow the gap, and they have been quite successful. Likewise, if there are many problems in the differential treatment of permanent versus temporary workers, instead of avoiding them or being disappointed that you're not able to resolve the problems immediately, you should continue to investigate ways to improve the situation. Only then will there be hope for progress on the issue.

However, leading a happy life should be your priority no matter what anyone else says. Your efforts for social change will have a greater ripple effect when you yourself are happy. If you have a positive attitude and get along well with others with a smile on your face, you'll receive a lot of support as you carry out social movements and participate in rallies.

However, even if we make efforts to make the world a better place, this doesn't mean that we'll be able to see the results right away. When we begin any project, we hope to see the results immediately, but the world doesn't work that way. Our efforts sometimes bear fruit, but other times, they don't. If they do, that's great, but if they don't, we can devise a different method and try again. If we fail despite our best efforts, then we must give up and try something else.

One thing you should keep in mind is that whatever you do, instead of doing it for the benefit of society and other people, you should do it because it's rewarding and fun for you. Then, you can be happy regardless of the outcome. If you succeed, you'll feel happy that your task was successful. But if you don't, it will be alright because you had fun in the process.

Many people think that if they don't succeed, it means they've failed, but that's not exactly true. There is no such thing as failure. If you start building something and lay the foundation before you die, your successors or descendants can build on it, and if they're unable to finish, others can continue the work.

Change takes time. If the goal is to bring about fundamental change, it will take a very long time. But if you set an easy goal, it can be achieved tomorrow.

Wanting to see something to completion because you're the one who started it's an urge that stems from greed. Likewise, putting in less effort or even disregarding something because you're not the one who initiated it may also originate from greed.

Avoid being overly proud of doing good deeds or imbuing too much meaning into it. Don't take yourself too seriously, and you'll be happy regardless of the outcome.

The world thinks caring for others is unquestionably good and calls it "altruistic." However, if you think that you're making an effort for others, you will want to be compensated, which will lead to resentment.

Therefore, rather than thinking that we are sacrificing for others, it's best to think that helping others is helping ourselves. This concept can be expressed with the Buddhist term "Jari-ita." It means that benefiting oneself is no different from benefiting others.

Flowers provide bees with nectar while bees help flowers bear fruit by carrying the pollen. Likewise, we must live a life that is good for us, as well as for others. When we all realize that helping others also benefits us, and we stop regarding those acts as sacrifices, we will be on the path to shared happiness.

PART 05

PRACTICE
BEING HAPPIER
TODAY THAN YESTERDAY

As we live our lives, all kinds of things happen. Sometimes, your loved ones die, and sometimes, people go bankrupt and lose all their money. You may even get stabbed in the back by a person you deeply cared for. Nothing occurs without reason. However, these events don't happen because it's God's will or because you committed sins in your past life. They aren't mere coincidences either. You just don't know the reason behind them.

It's the same with the weather. There are times when it hails in the summer, when it's warm like spring in the winter, and when it's cool like fall during the summer. However, on average, summer is a little hotter, and winter is a little colder. Similarly, if you have a pure heart and live with good intentions, there is a higher chance of good things happening to you. On the other hand, if you have an impure heart and live with malicious intentions, there is a higher chance of bad things happening to you.

Therefore, when a problem occurs, acknowledging and accepting what has already happened is the first step toward finding a solution. Willingly accept the consequences of your actions, but if you don't want to face such consequences again, you should never repeat the same actions. You need to find out the exact cause of those consequences and eliminate them. If we seek to find solutions by paying close attention to what causes the issues in our lives, instead of constantly running away from our problems, the process turns into a challenge rather than an ordeal.

Letting Go
of Judgments

We often see the world through a binary lens. We think to ourselves, "This is right; that is wrong" or "I'm right; you're wrong." That's why we're continually caught up in our own judgments and trapped by our own expectations.

Imagine a garden of flowers with all sorts of beautiful blossoms. They do not argue with one another or compete with one another. Imagine, however, that when you're looking at the garden, you think, "This rose is beautiful but why is that tulip so ugly?" The thought would not stop there but would continue as a stream of endless thoughts. You might think, "Maybe those who did good deeds in their previous lives became roses, and those who did bad things became tulips."

These kinds of beliefs are referred to as "past lives," "astrological signs," or "punishment from heaven," depending on your worldview. A rose is just a rose; a tulip is just a tulip. There is no hidden meaning, and neither is better nor worse than the other.

In our world, some people like roses, others like tulips, and still others like azaleas. People's tastes and preferences vary quite extensively. There is no way to separate good preferences from bad ones. When you approach these differences with an attitude of curiosity and discovery, conflicts and arguments simply do not arise.

I was invited to give a talk at Google in 2014, where a staff member asked this question: "This year has been especially complicated and hard to swallow. From the conflicts in the Middle East to the Ebola virus outbreak, it feels as if the whole universe is drawing to a close. What's really going on?"

These kinds of events have been happening for a long time, and they'll continue to happen. The world is not so complex. The world only seems complicated when we lack the capacity to understand the changes that are happening.

Take the conflicts in the Middle East, the attacks by the Islamic State in Iraq and Syria(ISIS), for example. Their actions are typical of a weak and desperate group of people. The solution, therefore, is not complicated. It can be found by addressing the unfairness at the source of their anger. Violent suppression, on the other hand, is effective only in the short term. These groups may appear to be defeated, but they resurge again, escalating conflicts. That's why we need a different method of dealing with them. Responding with violent force, as if it's a war between countries, has not solved the problem. A different kind of response is needed.

The first step is understanding human psychology. No matter how ridiculous their claims may sound, we need to investigate why they feel that they have to behave in such a manner. When we react emotionally, saying, "An eye for an eye, and a tooth for a tooth," and respond with violence of our own, the situation only deteriorates.

"We'll talk only after you beg for forgiveness." This is not the right attitude. Authentic dialogue requires a willingness to sit at the table without attaching conditions. The time to ask for an apology is after the dialogue. Requiring an apology beforehand undermines the willingness to talk.

For dialogue to work, the stronger party needs to take the first steps toward making concessions. Even when dealing with gangs and terrorists, approaching the situation gently is more effective than declaring war. When the more powerful side makes a concession, it's called embracing the weak. However, when the weaker party makes a concession, it's called submission and capitulation. They will feel humiliated, motivating them to resist to the bitter end. Therefore, in order to resolve conflicts, the side with more power needs to make concessions.

If we could see it from a larger perspective, we'd realize that the seeds of tragedy were sown long before the disputes erupted. That's why punishing the other side based on apparent reasons leaves the root causes of conflict unresolved. True peace requires understanding and acceptance of the unique and intrinsic qualities of people on the other side. When we accept reality and build systems that promote positive changes, we can resolve conflicts, making the world more harmonious. Judgements about past actions – about whether or not they conform to our moral standards – can take place later.

Much of the anger in the world arises because this order is

reversed. We usually don't start by seeking to understand the reality of the situation, but instead, we jump immediately to judgements about right and wrong based on our own standards. This process leads to arguments, aggression, and anger.

The same applies to individuals. Imagine that, while riding on a crowded bus, someone suddenly slaps you in the face. At first, you'd get angry and feel wronged. If you later found out that you had stepped on that person's foot and broke their toe, you'd feel differently. Then, even though you were slapped, you would say, "Oh no, I'm very sorry." However, if you never realized that you had stepped on their toe, you would protest angrily, saying, "Why did you slap me?" Then, that person would also get angrier, and the conflict would escalate.

There's a wiser way to deal with this type of situation. Before judging, look inside yourself and think about how your own actions may have contributed to the situation. You need to examine whether rejecting the other person based on your insistence of being right hurt that person and brought you trouble.

Looking for the cause within yourself will help you solve

both individual and social problems, while blaming others will not. Even if you don't find the root cause, refraining from emotional confrontation prevents the situation from getting worse. It won't be easy, but you need to make a rational choice, unhindered by emotions. This is not to say that you should blame yourself or that you should silently tolerate unfair treatment. Just don't let emotions carry you away and blind you from the essence of the problem.

Trying to get even for being treated unfairly solves nothing. Acting toward someone as if they're an enemy only results in turning that person into an actual enemy, and violence only begets more violence. Unfair treatment should be disclosed with the goal of preventing others from becoming the victims of similar treatment. This requires detachment from our own judgements. When disclosing a problem, it must be done thoroughly and persistently, free from the sway of pressure and temptations. To do this, you need both courage and wisdom.

When unfairness is disclosed in anger, your statements become reduced to the level of personal vengeance. As a result, this evolves into a lonely and painful battle in which others can't help you. If, detached from hatred and resentment, you act with the aim of resolving the problem for yourself as well as for posterity, there will be people who empathize with you and support you. Then, this process will both heal your own pain and bring changes that benefit the world.

Insightfulness,
the Wisdom of Seeing the Whole

When we look at something, we typically see it from just one angle. It could be from our own perspective as individuals, as parents, or as Koreans. However, we mistakenly think we understand the entirety of the issue. The result is that we mistake our biases for our convictions.

During a Dharma talk, someone might nod their head and say, "Yes, Sunim, that's right." Does this mean that they understood what I said? On the other hand, someone else might shake their head and say, "No, that's not true." Does that mean that they didn't understand? No, that's not what it means. It only signifies that the person who nods their head shares the same opinion as I do, while the person who shakes their head has a different opinion from mine.

We look at the world through distorted lenses, mistaking our biases for our convictions. Through these lenses, we judge what we see as right or wrong. It's as if we're wearing different colored glasses, thinking that whatever we see is really yellow, red, or blue. We're like the proverbial blind men touching different parts of an elephant. One touches the leg and says that the elephant is like a pillar; another touches the trunk and compares it to a snake. Each mistake is a part of the whole.

In the same way, we view the world based on the limited experience of our immediate surroundings and our own perspectives and say, "This is truth" or "This is right." In looking only at ourselves, we don't see our children, parents, or spouses as they really are. When we're looking at our home, we don't see our neighbors' homes. When we focus on our own country, we don't see other people's countries. When considering only our religion, we can't understand other people's religions. We're continually clinging to our own point of view while insisting that we are right.

When people ask me questions, it might seem like I'm

providing answers, but that's not what is really happening. I'm simply helping them to see the situation from a different angle. When someone approaches the situation from the front, I ask, "What does it look like from the back?" When somebody is looking at one side, I ask, "What's it like on the other side?" If they view it from the top, I ask, "What's going on at the bottom?" This is called "seeing the totality." Looking at something from a particular angle is called bias; seeing the whole is called insightfulness or wisdom.

When we let go of attachments based on one-sided perspectives, we see that what we considered problems aren't really problems. When we attain the wisdom of looking at the whole, many of our troubles simply disappear, just as the darkness in a dark room dissipates once the light is turned on.

To awaken is to open both eyes and see the whole, instead of only considering one side or going off your biases. It means overcoming prejudices and judgements based on a one-sided perception. To awaken is to see multiple perspectives simultaneously: it is to see others along with ourselves, others' homes as well as our own homes, others' religions along with our own, others' countries as well as our own, and the North along with the South. By looking at the whole, you can see the truth and follow the right path.

One day, a young man said that the world we live in seems very unfair. He asked me the following question: "Why am I only five foot seven(170cm) and so unattractive? Many men are over six feet(183cm) and handsome. And why are there people in the world who are wealthy while others are poor? Why are there people who are happy and people who are unhappy? Is this the law of nature? Is this the world that God and the Buddha spoke about?"

Why do we think that the conditions we have are unfair? If you were born a woman in a world where men are privileged and women oppressed, you would lament, "Why was I born a woman?" However, there is nothing inherently good or bad about being born as a man or as a woman. It's just that you were born into a society that gives privileges to men that are not granted to women. If a woman laments, "Why was I born a woman?" it's only because she doesn't have the same privileges as a man. If the custom of granting privileges based on gender were to disappear, this question wouldn't arise. Therefore, the social discrimination between women and men is the issue; being born a woman is neither wrong nor unfair.

Similarly, people with disabilities sometimes lament their situations because society causes them inconveniences and puts them at a disadvantage. However, the disability itself is neither wrong nor a punishment. Saying that those who were good in a past life are born into wealth is just a way for the privileged to rationalize their wealth.

In addressing problems people face in life, many false teachings have been propagated as part of religion. These range from, "It's a punishment for not believing in God," to "It's a punishment for sins committed in previous lives." However, Jesus and the Buddha actually instructed their followers not to discriminate against people of different genders, different skin colors, or different abilities.

Our present society tends to view tall people as more attractive and short people as less attractive and somewhat inferior. However, every height has both advantages and disadvantages. Some situations are advantageous for tall people; others are advantageous for short people. When one person is tall, and another person is short, the truth of the matter is that they have different heights. On the other hand, whether height causes attractiveness or unattractiveness is in the eye of the beholder. It has no basis in objective reality.

An elephant was not born big because of good deeds in its previous life; a mouse isn't small because of sins committed in its past life. There is no inequality in nature. Just because snakes eat frogs, it doesn't mean that a snake was born more superior than a frog. They're just different species.

Over the course of history, discrimination between the nobility and commoners has disappeared in Korea. That's why people no longer lament, "Why was I born a commoner?" By the same token, we need a revolutionary way of thinking about height, perhaps with the slogan, "Short is beautiful." Why on earth is being short a problem? From an environmental standpoint, being short has many advantages. It means that less material is needed for clothing. Beds can also be smaller. Since shorter people consume less, they can contribute to conserving resources and energy.

We need to consider whether or not our beliefs are accurate reflections of reality. Looking at something through our prejudices is like trying to find something by groping around in a dark room. Maybe we'll find it, and maybe we won't. We might bump into something and fall down. We might mistakenly grab hold of something else. However, when we turn on the light and see the entire room, we can find it immediately.

When we gain insight, we can see everything in the world as it really is. Then, the frantic mind, trying to decide whether something is right or wrong or whether to do this or that, quiets down. Your heart quickly becomes lighter. The darkness of your mind instantly gives way to light.

Therefore, we need to cultivate the wisdom to see the whole instead of clinging to society's stereotypes and fixed notions. Then we can live, not as slaves to our circumstances, but as masters of our own lives.

The Choice Between
Conflict Escalation and Mutual Benefit

Our social environment contribute significantly to our inability to see the whole picture and to getting caught up in biases. Korea is the only divided nation in the world. South and North Korea have yet to sign a peace treaty, so the possibility of war breaking out again still hangs over the Korean peninsula.

Even though a ceasefire lasting 70 years has desensitized most South Korean citizens to the threat of war, the continued division of the country has impeded the people from thinking freely. Thus, while talking about a social issue, if you have a different opinion from others, people may condemn you, saying, "That's a dangerous idea." Also, being confined within the framework of a divided nation, South Korea has experienced limitations in political, economic, and social development. Only when the two Koreas are reunified, demolishing the barrier that hinders open-mindedness, will we be able to think freely and exert our creative powers to design a brighter future.

We tend to envy the creative reasoning and philosophies of the Western world, but the West also experienced a dark age, called the Middle Ages. Any thought or speech that didn't conform to the religious principles of the time was greatly oppressed, and many lost their lives in religious inquisitions. People in the Western world had to undergo countless hardships before gaining the right to think freely. This experience didn't come without a cost.

A man once asked me the following question: "A while ago, when a war seemed imminent on the Korean peninsula, I had a conversation with my coworkers. They agreed that unification was necessary, but they didn't want it to happen during their lifetime. They said that they want our country to be unified after they've passed away. Personally, when I think about our current situation, I think it's better for the two Koreas to be unified as soon as possible. However, I don't know how to talk to those who have negative opinions on unification. What can I, as an ordinary citizen, do to contribute to the unification of the Korean peninsula?"

In return, I asked him, "Why do you think it's good for the two Koreas to become unified?"

"Well, first of all, by unifying, we will expand our territory. Currently, South Korea is isolated like an island, but when the two Koreas are unified, the country will become connected to continental Asia. Moreover, the national defense expenditure could be used for other purposes, which will help the country become more financially stable."

"You could say that to your coworkers."

"I did, and they said that they were against unification because they would have to pay more taxes. They also said that many North Koreans who can't make a living in North Korea will come to live in South Korea. As a result, there will be disorder in the South Korean society, and it's not clear what North Koreans may do in that situation.

They are correct in saying that, after unification, we'll have to pay more taxes and that there is a risk of social disorder due to many North Koreans relocating to South Korea.

First, there is a lot of controversy over the cost of unification because the money that would go into the development of North Korea is regarded as an expense. However, the resources that would go toward developing North Korea would actually be an investment. For instance, it costs money to develop the iron mines in Musan, North Korea. However, it's cheaper compared to importing iron ore from another country. After the initial investment to develop the mine, we will be able to obtain the iron for free. This is why China has invested one billion dollars into the Musan iron mine for the right to mine the iron for 30 years. If we were to unify with North Korea, we wouldn't have to pay one billion dollars for mining rights. North Korea has abundant reserves of rare earth minerals and precious metals such as gold, silver, and copper. It's estimated that North Korea has about 30 times more underground natural resources than South Korea.

Furthermore, if we view unification as having 20 million extra mouths to feed, it appears to be a huge and fruitless expenditure. However, think about the low-cost laborers we will gain. The monthly wage of a worker at Gaeseong Industrial Complex in North Korea is $150, and such cheap labor cannot be found even in China. The combination of the high-skill, low-cost workforce of North Korea and the capital and technology of South Korea will enable the reunified Korean nation to become a global production powerhouse. Essentially, the cost of unification comes down to how it's calculated. Employing an erroneous method of calculation makes people feel that the cost of unification is a burden.

It's best to cover North Korea's development costs with our own capital rather than borrowing from foreign countries and paying interest. To make this possible, we'll have to pay a little more in taxes. However, investing our own money into developing North Korea will yield large profits.

However, resistance is to be expected because people will not be able to immediately see the benefits of paying an extra $100 in taxes. Therefore, the public needs to be part of the discussion, and be persuaded if necessary, when figuring out the amount of additional taxes they may have to pay.

We should calculate how much more in taxes citizens need to pay for 10 years after reunification to help fund the development of North Korea and turn a profit. We also need to approximate how much profit the country will see. If an investment of $1,000 over 10 years gives a return of $5,000, it will be worth making the investment. If there is a shortage of development funds, or if it's too much of a burden for the citizens to pay the additional taxes, it's always possible to attract foreign capital to help cover the costs.

Unification could become a huge breakthrough for young people who've had to give up their life goals due to unemployment and are living in continual anxiety about the future. When large-scale investments for constructing roads, laying railway tracks, supplying electric power, planting trees and so on, take place in North Korea, South Korean industries will be revitalized. This will also influence the development of the three provinces of Dongbei, China, which shares a border with North Korea that is over 800 km long. The Dongbei provinces will become our market and supplier of resources. Furthermore, if the infrastructure and technology of Korea and Japan are combined with Siberia's resources and Dongbei's labor force, a new economic community centered in the East-Sea Rim Region may be formed, enabling the unified Korea to exert a significant influence in the region.

Likewise, there will be a drastic change in the mentality

of the young people, many of whom feel powerless today. Many teenagers today will tell you that their dream is to become a public official. The position of a public official should draw people who are concerned about public welfare, but young people are saying that they want to be a civil servant only because they prefer a stable job in the current economic uncertainty.

If the two Koreas should become unified, the Korean peninsula could become like Europe, where one can go across many different countries by train. We could take a train or bike all the way to Dongbei or Beijing in China, tour the maritime territory of Russia, go on a trip to Siberia, explore the historical land of Balhae, and travel to Mongolia. Then, young Koreans would have an expanded playing field and be able to dream bigger dreams.

Then, why aren't North Korea and South Korea actively pursuing unification? Let's say a married couple had a fight and are now living separately. It would be great if they conceded to each other and reconciled for the sake of their children, so that the family could live together. However, if the wife says to the husband, "If you got down on your knees and beg for forgiveness, I'd be willing to live with you again," and if the husband also demands the same thing from the wife, they will most likely end up getting a divorce. Likewise, the years of animosity between the two Koreas makes unification very difficult. Even though both sides know that unification will be beneficial, they can't reach a consensus because each side wants the upper hand.

My hope is that South Korea—the more powerful of the two—takes a magnanimous approach toward North Korea in resolving this issue. However, it's true that it's challenging to reach a consensus, even among South Koreans, because those whose feelings have been hurt by North Korea's past will react emotionally and protest, "Why should we be pushed around by the North Koreans?" And we need to understand why these people react the way they do.

We need to recognize that we are living in critical times. Currently, we have the opportunity to create a new world, so we must view the issue of inter-Korean relations with a balanced perspective. We must remember that the choices we make today will not only impact the current generation but will also decide the fate of our future generations.

Getting angry and rejecting North Korea because we find their behavior detestable is an emotional choice rather than a rational one. It would be great if we could change them by beating them up, but that could result in a backlash and lead to war. Another possibility is that North Korea could rely more on China and eventually become subjugated to China. If that happens, unification with North Korea will no longer be possible, and this would be a tremendous loss for South Korea in the long run.

We have to choose whether to suffer losses by escalating conflict or to get on the path to prosperity together. Of course, before we can make that choice, we first need to evaluate the situation thoroughly and objectively. The reality is that South Korea and North Korea have had guns aimed at each other for a long time.

Considering the conflict between the two sides over the years, those who insist "North Koreans are our brothers and sisters" are idealists, while those who argue, "North Koreans are our sworn enemies" are being complacent. South Korea and North Korea are hostile to each other, but if we want unification, we can only be unified with North Korea. It's not like South Korea can be unified with the U.S. or with Japan. In other words, North Korea is both our sworn enemy as well as our kin.

We must acknowledge the fact that even though North Korea is our future partner for unification, currently we are in an antagonistic relationship. Thus, while we should continue to take a firm and uncompromising stance against North Korea's threats, we can also cooperate on economic matters that benefit each other, separate from political or military matters. Also, providing humanitarian aid to North Korea should be considered purely from a humanitarian perspective unrelated to politico-military issues. It's true that the human rights situation in North Korea is dire and needs to be improved, but we can't demand that they meet South Korean standards overnight. The human rights situation must be gradually improved in accordance with North Korea's current reality.

We need to approach the issue from a broader perspective that goes beyond those of conservatives or liberals. People in South Korea don't want to go to war with North Korea, but they also don't want to be bullied and ordered around. If we only talk about economic cooperation with North Korea while not taking any measures against their threats, people might worry that South Korea is being pushed around by North Korea. On the other hand, if the South Korean government pushes for a strong retaliation each time North Korea provokes South Korea, people will be anxious and concerned that war might be just around the corner. Thus, if South Korea deals firmly with North Korea's intimidation tactics while continuing to promote economic cooperation on a regular basis, people will be less worried about war breaking out.

We'll be able to get one step closer to peace when we recognize the uniqueness of the other side and respond accordingly. That doesn't mean we're being servile or being dragged around. It means we are moving toward something greater. It's the best way to resolve conflict and maintain peace, leading to mutual benefit.

The Merit of
Comforting Others

In August 1996, the barrier that divided South Korea and North Korea in my heart fell thanks to an incident that occurred during a historical tour in China. Our young Korean-Chinese guide asked me for help, saying, "North Korean children are starving to death." He pleaded with me several times, but I didn't believe him because I thought it was nonsense.

Since he kept telling me, "It's true. Go and see it for yourself," I boarded a boat on the Amnokgang River, still thinking that this couldn't be true. However, on the North Korean side of the river, I saw emaciated children sitting feebly on the ground. I was shocked and called out to them, but they didn't raise their heads.

Usually, hungry children will follow strangers around to try and obtain anything they can get, even just a piece of candy, so it was strange that these kids were so unresponsive. The young guide explained that North Korean children never beg to outsiders even if they're hungry because they were taught from a very young age not to disgrace their country. So, I tried to throw the food I had with me to the riverbank. However, the guide stopped me, saying, "You can't do that because we are at the China-North Korea border."

My heart ached. Even birds fly across the river to find food on the other side. So I was appalled that I couldn't hand food over to people who were dying of starvation just because we were divided by a border. After all, nations are formed to benefit people.

I became painfully aware of the harsh reality of a divided nation. I couldn't help the starving children of my own Korean kin, who were only a few meters away, but I could go abroad to help children of faraway nations like India and the Philippines.

From that point on, the wall that divided the two Koreas

in my mind tumbled down. Since that day, I have not been able to stop helping the North Korean people, no matter how much suspicion and criticism are pointed my way.

I adhere to three principles when helping people who are in need: "The hungry should have food; the sick should be treated; children should be educated."

Such principles are reflected in the last words of the Buddha. When Ananda asked the Buddha, "After you pass away, to whom can we make offerings to accumulate merit?" The Buddha said, "There are four types of offerings that are as honorable as the offerings made to me. First is to feed the hungry, second is to treat the sick, third is to help and comfort the poor and lonely, and fourth is to protect the pure-minded practitioners."

Currently, on Earth, there are many people starving to death or suffering from severe malnutrition. Among the nearly 8 billion people around the world today, almost 10% are estimated to be living in extreme poverty and living on less than $1.90 a day.

These people suffer from severe malnutrition and cannot dream of receiving medical care, let alone sending their children to school. Diseases that are easily treatable, such as paratyphoid fever, only cost a few dollars to treat in South Korea. Tuberculosis costs less than $100 to treat, but the extremely poor can't afford it. Therefore, if they contract the disease, they have no choice but to await death. Almost 10 percent of people in the world suffer from such extreme poverty.

Between 1995 and 1998, about 3 million people died of hunger and disease in North Korea. The death of this many people means that those who survived also suffered greatly as they watched their family members and neighbors die.

When we hear about those who are suffering, we generally respond in two ways. One is avoidance. People who respond this way are those who can't understand the suffering of others until they experience it themselves. The other group consists of those who become distressed and worry all the time. Empathizing with other people's suffering may seem better than ignoring it, but the people who respond in these two ways are basically the same because they are caught up in their own thoughts. Neither response is really helpful to the people who are suffering.

After I saw the starving North Korean children, I went around crying. They looked so destitute. It would be hard for those who haven't seen them with their own eyes to believe it.

When you're participating in humanitarian relief work, you sometimes feel angry because of people's indifference, and sometimes you become deeply saddened because you feel powerless. However, being sad doesn't help the suffering people in any way and doesn't change anything. It only makes your own heart ache.

Therefore, instead of falling into distress when you see people suffering, you should look for ways to help, even just one of them, and be thankful that you are still healthy and able to earn a living. Rather than worrying all night about the people who are suffering and wallowing in sadness, it's better to get a good night's sleep and try to find ways to actually help them.

When I ask others to help the needy, I often hear the following responses: "It's hard enough for me to make a living. How can I possibly help others?" "There are so many poor people in South Korea. Shouldn't we help them first?" "Would my small donation make a difference?"

When there are ten people who need help, but you can only help one, you'll feel powerless. However, you just need to do what you can with what you have even if you are only able to help one or two people.

Do you think there are only ten people who need help in this world? Of course not. There are hundreds, thousands, and many more. Counting the number of people who need help and lamenting your inability to assist them all will only make you miserable. If you can help one person, go ahead. And if you're able to help two, you can do that. Just do what you can.

It's good to aspire to gain the ability to help more people. If you set an aspirational goal that is not rooted in greed or ego, you'll build your capacity to help ten people even if you can only help one person now. If you set a more ambitious aspiration, you may be able to help a hundred people by finding new ways to make it possible. This is because your sincere dedication will move the hearts of the people around you. Then, unexpected miracles can occur.

When we set out to help others, we are repaid many times over with the happiness we feel. However, many people think that they will be happy when they receive something from others. This is because we have been brainwashed to think that way since birth.

If you live with the belief that happiness comes from receiving, you'll continue to seek external blessings and keep wanting more even if you become economically affluent. Then, you won't be able to stop feeling poor all your life. If you're lucky, you may enjoy temporary happiness, but it won't last.

For example, let's suppose that a friend of yours gives you $1,000 every month. Would happiness be the only thing you feel? How would you feel whenever you meet that friend to receive the money? You'd probably feel very small in front of them and take care not to offend them. It would be difficult to refuse what they ask you to do regardless of whether it was beyond your abilities or morally wrong.

Those who like receiving help depend on others. With time, when these people become financially stable, they often don't want to keep in touch with those who helped them when they were struggling. This is because they don't want their past to be revealed.

If you want to realize your wish of receiving things from others, you need to be in a situation that requires the help of others. This means that you have to become miserable, poor, or sick. In short, those who like to receive help make themselves pitiful.

This is not limited to material things. If you want to get things, whatever they may be, you will always feel that it's not enough, no matter how much you receive. You'll feel happy only temporarily when you receive something, but the happiness won't last long.

On the other hand, if you give and share, you'll feel rich regardless of how much you possess. You don't have to give something big. You can just give whatever you're able to share.

Giving a meal to a hungry person, giving clothes to a person who needs them, and helping a child that has fallen down get back up are all acts of giving. As you continue giving, you'll find out that you end up benefiting much more than you gave.

We all suffer from various difficulties in life. However, when we look around, there are many people who live each day in distress without basic necessities. When we understand their pain and try to comfort and help them, our problems become smaller and lighter. You realize, "Wow, my problem is nothing compared to theirs. I'm a happy person with many blessings after all."

When you help others, you change from a person who used to dwell on trivial things and suffered as a result into someone who feels grateful and happy. This is the merit of helping others.

Different Levels
of Love

Every January, I lead a pilgrimage to India, retracing the footsteps of the Buddha. On the pilgrimage, we always encounter children begging. They stretch out their dirty hands, saying "Baksheesh, baksheesh." Soft-hearted Korean pilgrims take pity on them, rummage through their pockets, and hand each child a one-rupee coin.

Somehow, as time passes, those who felt sorry for the children and willingly gave them coins at first start to feel annoyed. It's because the children come back to get more instead of leaving after getting one. "I gave you a coin already." "Don't give it to him. He got one from me just now." They fuss like this. The coin they give is worth about 10 cents. After giving one coin, they get upset if the children try to get more than one. This is our level of helping others.

We make up our minds to help others, but it's not easy to maintain this mindset regardless of our circumstances and conditions. For this to be possible, we must have, in Christian terms, the "Love of Jesus" in our hearts. In Buddhist terms, we need the heart of a bodhisattva.

Kshitigarbha is a bodhisattva who vowed to save all sentient beings in hell. Kshitigarbha goes down to hell to endlessly save all sentient beings. Even if someone he has previously saved returns to hell, Kshitigarbha never gives up and saves them again.

It would be difficult enough to save someone who is in hell. If that same person returns to hell two or three times after making the same mistakes, most of us would say to ourselves, "I already saved them; I don't need to save them again!" After saving someone who is in hell, if we saw that person there again, we'd likely give up on the idea of saving them for the second time. This is our level of compassion. Kshitigarbha's compassion, on the other hand, is boundless. He maintains his vow to save all sentient beings and keeps saving them no matter how many times they fall back into hell.

I began to help the Dalits (people belonging to the lowest caste) in India after an experience I had during my first pilgrimage there in 1991. On my first night in Calcutta, I went out to buy some water, and I encountered a young woman begging with a baby in her arms. The moment she saw me, she grabbed my garment and led me to a small store, where she pointed to a can of baby formula that she wanted me to buy for her. I asked the shopkeeper for the price. It was 60 rupees.

At that moment I remembered some advice I had received before traveling to India. I'd been advised not to give more than one rupee to any begging child since one rupee was a substantial amount in India. Based on this advice, 60 rupees sounded like a lot of money. I was startled by the price, so I left the shop without buying the baby formula for the young woman.

After buying the two bottles of water I needed, I returned to the hotel, where I asked my travel guide how much 60 rupees was worth in Korean won. He said that it was about 2,400 KRW, or about 2 USD. This made me feel terrible.

She had asked me to buy her a can of baby formula that cost only $2, and I reacted as though she had asked me to hand over all of my possessions.

I had participated in various social movements and urged people to help the poor. At Buddhist temples, I talked to people about the need to alleviate human suffering, and yet I had turned away from real suffering that was happening right in front of my own eyes. I was utterly shocked by my contradictory behavior.

After this shocking realization, I gave away my extra clothes and most of the money that I had with me. Subsequently, many more children began following me around, and my fellow travelers complained a great deal.

Days later, we came upon a village in the countryside, where I saw a small group of children sitting together. I called out to offer them some candy, but instead of coming to take the candy, they ran away. Once again, I was shocked.

In my encounter with the young woman begging to buy formula for her baby, the problem was that I had refused to help. After the episode with the children who refused my offer of candy, I realized that the children begged because travelers kept giving them things, not because of their poverty. The children in the countryside were just as poor, but because nobody ever gave them anything, they didn't beg. When I tried to give them candy, the children became shy and ran away. I came to the conclusion that it was the travelers who caused the children to beg. Realizing that giving was not necessarily always good, I decided not to give anything more to any begging children.

Later, on my way to the Sujata Temple near Bodh Gaya, I passed a young boy begging on the street; he had no legs. When I refused, he followed me, dragging himself with his hands for more than a kilometer.

I began to question whether I was doing the right thing in not giving anything to a child who had made such an effort to get, at least, a ballpoint pen, a stick of gum, or a piece of candy. I began to doubt myself. Once again, my perspective changed.

I concluded that the real issue wasn't the children's attitudes; it was mine. I started to reflect on how I could help children without turning them into beggars. I eventually built a school, a hospital, and wells for the Dalits in Dungeshwari, India. Thanks to my mistakes and my efforts to correct them, I gained an opportunity to do something good.

Had I simply been generous from the start, I would never have thought of building a school in India. This is why making mistakes isn't necessarily a bad thing. When we recognize our mistakes and repent, we may end up developing true love and compassion for others.

Happiness Lies in Doing Something Fun and Rewarding

Today, South Korea is better off economically, and we're more open-minded than before, but we haven't changed much in the sense that we are still tied down to something. In the past, people were tied down to class or land as slaves or serfs. Now, we're tied down to money in a capitalist society. Whether we are tied down to class, land, or money, it's the same in that we are tied down to something.

There are two types of situations where people feel happy. We feel happy when we're doing something we want to do and when we are contributing in some way to the welfare of others. However, if we only pursue what feels good in the present, we may regret it or feel empty later on. On the other hand, if we focus too much on future benefits, we may experience hardship in our present lives and become weary. The best option is to balance the two and do things that we can enjoy in the present and will also benefit us in the future. We should benefit others as well as ourselves. To make this possible, there shouldn't be a gap between what we enjoy doing and what is beneficial to others. If we consider helping others part of our job and have fun while working, we won't need to go somewhere else after work to relieve stress.

There are many ways we can live our lives. In my case, I try to donate my time, energy, and resources to places where they can be most beneficial. For example, there is little you can buy with 1,000 KRW or 1 USD in Korea. Yet the same amount of money can feed five children in India. That dollar is worth a lot more in India than in South Korea or the U.S., so it's more rewarding to spend the same amount of money to help the people in India. Essentially, I seek out locations with the most suffering and hardship, because I can help a great number of people and because it feels much more gratifying as well.

People generally want to go to heaven or paradise, but I do

not share that desire. They say heaven is a good place, which means I wouldn't have much to do there. On the other hand, if I go to hell, I'll have plenty of work to do. Since my limited abilities will be useful there, I'm sure I'll find it more fun and rewarding. Therefore, when Christians spreading the gospel on the street tell me, "If you don't believe in Jesus, you'll go to hell," I say, "Thank you."

Whoever you are, you have unique talents and abilities that enable you to do things that you both like to do and can do well. Just ask yourself where your talents are most needed and where they can be most effective. Using your abilities effectively makes the experience more enjoyable and rewarding, enabling you to become more self-confident. Negative thoughts, such as "I'm a useless person," or "Should I just die?" would never occur to you. When you approach life with an attitude focused on how you can better help others, you'll feel and look more energized.

Using your talents in an effective manner is also related to choosing a job. In the past, it was hard to make a living, and people's career options were more limited. Back then, the goal was just to find a job with a higher salary. If you succeeded in snagging the position, you were also expected to fulfill higher expectations, resulting in a heavy workload. Also, your spending increased because you had to meet the rising expectations and demands of your family and friends. Consequently, even if your job was tough and you hated it, you couldn't afford to quit, so you had to lead an exhausting life.

However, you don't have to continue living that way. As long as you can earn enough to live on, it's wiser for you to choose work that you find both fun and rewarding. When you let go of your desire to work in certain corporations and the desire for status, and instead, seek to become a person who is needed in this world, you'll become happy and make a positive impact on the world.

I don't accept compensation for my Dharma talks. If I was paid, it would be labor, but since I don't, it's volunteer work. When people are forced to work without compensation, we call it "slavery." When they're paid for their work, we call it "labor." Similarly, if people are promised $100 in return for a certain amount of work but are only paid $50, this is considered exploitation. However, if they don't expect compensation but do it for the good of the world, we call it volunteering. Therefore, when you choose a job with low pay and a high workload, it's similar to volunteering.

On the other hand, if you have a job with a high salary but a light workload, you are living an indebted life. In this respect, volunteer work, making use of our abilities to the fullest without pay, is the most advanced form of labor and the path to true freedom.

In the future, the world will be more appreciative of people who choose jobs based on their interest or how much they can contribute to the world rather than how much they can earn. They are happy people who shine wherever they are. In this sense, the significant increase in the number of people donating their talents and volunteering is a positive phenomenon.

When you know there are places that need you, where you can be highly useful, you can dispel long-standing self-doubt and discover the true value of your life. True happiness begins when you no longer obsess about money. Instead of focusing on how much money you can make, you should base your decisions on where your efforts will be the most useful. It's worthwhile to realize your dreams and ideals even if you have to spend your own money to do so. After all, true happiness lies in doing something fun and rewarding.

How to Organize Your Time to
Live Happily

Once, a woman asked me how she could attain self-actualization, saying that she felt apathetic: "I've held jobs and had various experiences, but I haven't been able to feel satisfied. Since my children began going to school, I have more free time, but I'm not happy, and I keep thinking about the reason for it. It occurred to me that I've lived without a dream for some time. What do I need to do to pursue my dream?"

Having a job outside the home and earning money is not the only way to attain self-actualization. If your spouse is making enough money to support your family, you don't need to earn extra just to buy expensive clothes or live in a bigger house. Instead, you can volunteer at places like churches or temples, doing things like cooking, cleaning, or serving lunch to the hungry. Then, your spirit may improve, and your face will glow with new energy and vigor.

If you do that, you're less likely to be bothered by trivial things. So, you might not nag your spouse to come home earlier or scold your children to get better grades. When you aren't doing anything worthwhile with your life, you may be easily dominated by the smallest desires.

When you use your free time to volunteer, while taking care of your family, you'll feel grateful to your spouse as his income enables you to do it. As a result, when you return from a day of volunteering, for example, you're likely to take more care in preparing dinner for your family.

However, you don't have to feel inferior to your spouse because he's earning an income and you are not. When you volunteer as much as your schedule permits, that will enable you to attain self-actualization. On the other hand, forcing yourself into a job just to make some extra money is akin to enslaving yourself for money.

There are three things you can do to take the path toward

self-actualization. The first is donating money to the poor. The second is expressing gratitude during prayer instead of asking for good fortune. The third is doing volunteer work in gratitude for the blessings you have already received. Then, you'll naturally attain the self-actualization you are seeking.

If you volunteer for about three years, you'll become much happier and more emotionally stable. Then, you can seek employment if that's what you want. After you have worked hard as a volunteer without any pay, you'll be happy and at ease no matter what kind of job you have. However, instead of taking my advice, if you are determined to get a job under the belief that you can self-actualize only by having an enviable career, you will be constantly under pressure, perpetuating your suffering.

When I say that you should volunteer and contribute to society, this doesn't mean that you should go to extremes, abandoning your marriage and giving away all your money to join a monastic order. You don't need to participate in social movements at the risk of going to jail. What I mean is that, if you have 100 units of time, you can spend 80 of them on your own affairs and the other 20 on addressing global issues and doing what is needed in our society. That way, you can lead your own life that includes jobs and marriage, as well as volunteering.

If you spend twenty percent of your time volunteering, your life will become significantly better. When you do something rewarding, it invigorates your life, enabling you to accomplish more during the remaining eighty percent. Then, whether you're washing the dishes, cleaning the bathroom, or working at your job, you'll be able to lead a happy life wherever and whenever.

What does it mean to set aside part of your time and make good use of it? At Google, they have what they call the 20% Project. Based on this system, employees are able to freely use 20% of their work time on whatever they are interested in. Surprisingly, most of the major products and services of the company have actually been developed during this 20% free time.

It may be a coincidence, but the reason I began to focus on global issues such as the environment, poverty, and peace was thanks to the conclusion I arrived at after investing part of my time in reflecting deeply about future concerns. My colleagues and I asked ourselves, "Are we too focused on current issues? We need to explore new paths." Thirty years ago, I asked my colleagues to set aside their current projects to freely explore new issues.

After one year of much deliberation, we were able to narrow the topics down to three prominent issues: the environmental issue, at the global level; the poverty issue in developing countries, at the panhuman level; and peace and unification on the Korean peninsula, at the national level. In addition, we agreed that at the individual level, practice was the most important.

Before tackling these issues in earnest, I went to a temple to reflect on the task ahead while working as a manual laborer. This gave me time to let go of my focus on current issues and explore how best to proceed.

At that time, our decision to put aside existing issues was met with criticism. However, after 30 years, we are now being commended for taking a lead on environmental protection, relief aid, and unification efforts.

The time and effort invested that year recharged us and transformed our lives. It also proved that we can achieve better results when we attempt things freely outside of the established framework rather than just working hard on pressing issues.

When we're busy running around all day, like a hamster on a treadmill, we feel like there's never enough time. That's why, when I suggest using part of their time on new tasks, people often retort, "I need to support my family, and I don't even have enough time to sleep. How can I find the time?"

In the beginning, you don't need to spare a lot of time. Start with only one hour a day and increase the time gradually. You'll be able to find the time if you make up your mind to do so. You can use your free time, reduce your working hours, or decrease the amount of time you spend shopping or watching television.

If you want to experience genuine joy and happiness, you need to make your life worthwhile. Difficulties won't necessarily make you unhappy. If you feel fulfilled, you'll be happy inside despite experiencing external hardships. When you use your time the way you choose to and can help others at the same time, you'll feel proud and fulfilled, which will naturally make you happy.

We Can Choose to
Be Happy at Any Moment

We often convince ourselves that our unhappiness is inevitable. However, regardless of our external circumstances, we have the right to be happy, and we can choose to be happy.

Regardless of whether your mother abandoned you, you got divorced, or your spouse had an affair, you have a right to be happy. However, many of us give ourselves plenty of reasons to justify our unhappiness.

I have a competitive advantage in life in that I am happier than other people. It's not because I have more skills or because I was born with more talent. Although I'm not married, I'm happier than a lot of people who are married.

I'm also happier than many people who are younger or healthier than I am. You need to have something that makes you happier than others.

None of us are perfect, so we all sometimes become irritated, angry, or greedy. However, regardless of our shortcomings, we should be positive and think, "Yes, I get irritated, but I get less irritated than you. I also experience suffering, but I experience suffering less than you."

After all, who is responsible for your happiness or unhappiness? In every situation, you are the one who is completely responsible. No one else can share this responsibility. Even if you fail an important exam, break up with a romantic partner, or lose a loved one, you can lead a happy life. Regardless of your situation, insisting that you can't help but suffer is a waste of your life.

No matter what troubles you may face, you have the right to be happy. Use this as a guiding principle of your life. Don't hand over responsibility for your life to your spouse or even to a deity. Please remember that you are the one who has control over your happiness and unhappiness in your life.

Here is what the Buddha said on this topic: "I am the one who creates my own happiness. I am the one who creates my own unhappiness. Nobody creates my happiness or unhappiness except for me."

In your relationship with your country or society, the same principle applies. No matter where you live, you're not a guest but the master of your own country.

Do you think you'll become happy if you emigrate to another country because you're unhappy in the one where you currently live? When you live in your country, you may think that you will be happy once you emigrate to another country, but once you get there, you realize that this is not the case. Likewise, high schoolers think their troubles will be over once they are accepted into college, but that's not the case either. Young people may think that their problems will be solved once they get married, but marriage brings plenty of problems of its own. Parents think they won't have anything to worry about when their children become adults, but they keep worrying even after their children leave the nest. This is the reality of human life.

We think, "When I get this, I will be happy. When I attain that, I will be free." We fervently believe this to be true, but it's far from reality.

Whatever circumstances you find yourself in, you should

be able to be happy and free in the here and now. Otherwise, you'll never be happy or free. There are many who just dream of happiness only to die without ever experiencing it. Instead of dreaming about happiness, you need to experience it.

Let go of the heavy burdens you carry and turn your eyes to other people's pain and difficulties. Volunteer several hours a week or multiple days a year and use your talents to help others without expecting anything in return. When, instead of focusing on personal gain and success, we live our lives with the aim of being someone who helps others and is needed in the world, we ourselves become happy while also benefiting the world. This is the way we can exercise our right to be happy. We can choose to be happy at any moment.

About the Author
Ven. Pomnyun Sunim

Ven. Pomnyun Sunim is a peace activist who delivers messages of peace and reconciliation, a humanitarian activist who provides various forms of aid to developing countries, a thinker who is paving the way toward a new alternative civilization, and an awakened practitioner. In 1988, he founded the Jungto Society, a community of practitioners who vowed to free themselves from suffering and devote themselves to serving others and the world by leading the life of a bodhisattva.

Ven. Pomnyun Sunim's Dharma talks are clear and straightforward. He has an exceptional ability to explain the Buddha's teachings in simple, contemporary language. As a result, his spoken and written messages go straight to the heart of the matter and enable people to redirect their eyes inward and self-reflect. Furthermore, the esoteric content of Buddhist sutras come to life through his wisdom, intuition, and insight.

As of April 2022, YouTube videos of Sumin's Dharma talks have had more than 1.7 billion views. He shares his wisdom with the general public on how to free themselves from suffering and how to become happy through his Dharma Q&As and the Happiness School program. To date, he has delivered more than 12,000 Dharma Q&As in South Korea and about 300 Dharma Q&As in other countries around the world, including the 115 talks he gave during his global tour in 2014. Also, since the Covid-19 pandemic began in 2020, Ven. Pomnyun Sunim has been interacting with hundreds of thousands of people through his weekly online Dharma Q&As in Korean, and bi-weekly talks in English. (See his website: https://pomnyun.com/)

Among the more than 50 books Ven. Pomnyun Sunim has published in Korean so far, the most notable are *Things Are Good as They Are Now, Buddha*, and *Commentary on the Diamond Sutra*. His books encompass

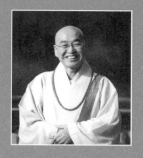

a wide range of subjects. His books, *Words of Wisdom for Newlyweds*, *Becoming Happier*, and *I Am a Decent Person*, provide insightful advice to young people. *Lessons for Life* is a guidebook for people living in modern society. *Prayer: Letting Go* is a manual for lay practitioners. *Practice Guidebook for Teachers* imparts wisdom for teachers. *The River of Life Flows* discusses an alternative solution to the environmental problem. And *Why Is Unification Necessary?* offers a vision for peace and unification on the Korean peninsula.

Some of these books have been translated into other languages, such as English, French, Thai, Japanese, Chinese, and Vietnamese. Eight books have been translated into English, including *Awakening*, *True Freedom*, *Prayer*, and *Monk's Reply to Everyday Problems* to list a few. Six books have been translated into Chinese, 3 books into Thai, 2 books into Japanese, 2 books into Vietnamese, and 1 book into French. Among the few books that were translated into multiple languages is *My Happy Way to Work*, which was translated into Thai, Chinese, Japanese, and Vietnamese. Another is *Becoming Happier*, which has English, Vietnamese, and Japanese versions.

Based on the idea that practice at the individual level goes hand in hand with social engagement, Ven. Pomnyun Sunim has engaged in extensive peace initiatives for various causes including a peaceful unification of the Korean Peninsula, refugee support, international relief efforts, and interfaith reconciliation and cooperation. Throughout the years, he has received numerous awards in recognition for his efforts. In 2002, he received the Ramon Magsaysay Award for Peace and International Understanding, and he was presented the 37th Niwano Peace Prize in 2021.

행복

VEN. POMNYUN SUNIM
BECOMING HAPPIER